the secret keepers

The Crystal Coast Series

the seCret keePers

Chrissy Lessey

Tenacious Books Publishing

Published by Tenacious Books Publishing

Copyright © 2019 Chrissy Lessey

Published in 2019 by Tenacious Books Publishing

tenacious@tenaciousbookspublishing.com

This book is a work of fiction. Names, characters, places, and incidents are either the product of the author's imagination or are used fictitiously.

Library of Congress Cataloging-in-Publication Data

The Secret Keepers / Chrissy Lessey

ISBN 9781733897419 (e-book)

ISBN 978-1-7338974-2-6 (print)

Cover Image: © iStock

Cover Design: Anita B. Carroll www.race-point.com

Book Design: Erin Rhew www.erinrhewbooks.com

Printed in the United States of America

www.tenaciousbookspublishing.com

For Amber

Chapter One

June 1718

Charlotte stood barefoot in the white sand, relishing the warmth of the summer sun. The sea, a sheet of deep green glass, sparkled with golden rays as a far-off vessel sailed across the horizon. Whether it carried pirates or merchants, she couldn't tell from so great a distance. Whatever the case, it didn't matter to her. She spared little thought for the men aboard that ship.

They didn't deserve her concern. Those men, regardless of whether they were pirates or merchants, would kill her without a second thought if they knew her secret.

But the cruelty of the mainland dwellers had driven her people to seek safety on the island, and for that part, Charlotte was grateful. Shifting her gaze to the fluffy clouds above, she inhaled the salty air with a smile. She couldn't imagine living anywhere other than the island, surrounded by men, women, and children who all shared the same gift. They worked together, trained together, and stayed safe together. Always.

A gusty wind blew in from the north, pulling loose strands from her braid and cooling her skin. When she turned into it, to feel the breeze against her face, she spotted her mother heading her way. Lucia walked with her usual determination, keeping her back straight and chin held high. Eyeing the large basket propped against her hip, Charlotte suspected her mother's current mission involved a food delivery of some sort.

It seemed a strange chore for such a powerful queen, but Charlotte had seen her do it time and again. Lucia had the respect and admiration of all who lived on the island, but it was her thoughtful, personal gestures—like this—that had earned their love.

One day, Charlotte would be queen. That day was far, far off, but when the time inevitably came, she hoped that she would be able to lead the same way her mother always had. She already had magic, but she desired wisdom. And long ago, Lucia had informed her that particular attribute would take nothing short of time and experience.

Stepping forward, she met Lucia midway and gestured toward the basket. "Dinner for the fishermen?"

The breeze kicked up once more, flapping their simple linen dresses against their legs.

"Just biscuits. I heard our traders have returned." Lucia shifted the basket to her other hand. "They'll be busy unloading supplies. This will hold them over until they can get a proper meal."

"Here, I can carry it." Charlotte reached forward to relieve her mother of the burden. "I'm going that way anyway."

Lucia laughed. "I doubt that's true. However, I'll gladly accept the help."

With matching strides, they continued walking together across the warm, soft sand toward the dock. Along the way, they passed a group of young women gathered in a circle, giggling loudly. Charlotte tilted her head at the curious sight.

Suddenly, the circle opened and out popped Sarah, who, unlike the others, wore something very different from the simple shifts favored by the women of the island.

Sarah twirled around to show off her new striped gown. With a thick, full skirt, it looked nothing short of torturous in the summer heat. Charlotte cringed at the sight of the too tight corset and imagined the pressure of the waist cincher's stays against her own ribcage. Why would anyone wear such a contraption of their own volition?

Sarah extended her arms. "Isn't it beautiful?"

"That's not the word I'd use to describe it," Charlotte muttered as she smiled and gave Sarah an approving nod.

Lucia laughed. "It seems our traders brought back more than just the essentials on this trip. Though I hope they only brought one of those dresses. Otherwise, we'll have a plague of modern fashion on our island."

"I'm perfectly happy with this." Charlotte looked down at her shapeless linen dress. "It's perfect for fishing, grinding flour, playing with the little ones…whatever I need to do. And, I can *breathe* in it."

They continued toward the dock. "Oh, but it's barely more than a nightgown to the mainlanders. They'd be quite taken aback by our state of undress here." She smirked.

"Undress? But I'm completely covered in this." With long, loose sleeves and a modest, rounded neckline, her shift could hardly be considered scandalous.

"It's still very different from the pretty prison that Sarah is wearing right now."

"Then it's a good thing those mainlanders aren't here because I wouldn't wear such a thing." The more Charlotte learned about the outside world, the more thankful she was for the freedom they had on the island.

"Yes. Indeed." Lucia glanced toward the ocean and her smile faltered when she spotted the large boat on the horizon. "Another ship?"

Charlotte nodded. "Yes. I noticed it just a bit ago. I don't think it's the same one I saw yesterday, but I couldn't say for certain from this distance."

She viewed the vast expanse of water, mirroring her mother's actions. To passing ships, their settlement would appear to be nothing more than a remote fishing village. A few primitive cottages, a dock, and some nets. Nothing remarkable. Nothing worth pillaging. Their people had lived and thrived in this humble kingdom since before Charlotte was born. But she knew it had always been a tenuous peace. A peace as unpredictable as the sea itself. The queen reminded her of that fact with increasing frequency as the years ticked by, as if their joyous existence held a time limit.

"I worry this will become a highly trafficked area. For so long, we were alone out here, and I knew we were safe—at least for a while." Lucia's brow creased. "But now…"

A knot formed in Charlotte's stomach as she watched her mother's expression darken. "Have you had a vision?"

Lucia reached up to touch the enormous teardrop amethyst that hung from the gold chain around her neck. As the most powerful member of their clan, she possessed a foresight the others didn't. The same gift that presented in Charlotte as little more than nagging, anxious feelings existed within her mother in the form of clear—though sometimes fractured—visions of the future. The queen's amulet no doubt played a role in the clarity of her premonitions, just as it offered her glimpses of the memories of the queens who had worn it before—in long past eras and faraway places.

Waiting for a reply, she watched her mother's graying hair shudder in the breeze. Lucia had once told her that wearing the pendant allowed the queens from the past to whisper in her ear. An exaggeration, Charlotte had always assumed. But as those deep lines stretched across her mother's forehead, she found herself questioning that assumption.

Charlotte did not have to hear the old stories to know that atrocities had befallen their ancestors. Those facts were evident every time she glimpsed Lucia's careworn face and every time her mother warned her to be careful.

Never practice within view of a boat. Always keep your magic invisible. Never show them what you are.

Hers had been a life full of "always" and "never." Still, she thought it had to be better than living among the mainlanders.

Lucia's graying hair shuddered in the breeze. "I haven't had a new vision, but I…"

"You've always worried so much, Mother. Maybe you're just on edge because of what you experienced in Salem Village? That's understandable." Charlotte stroked her arm. "But it was a *long* time ago."

"That may be the case in some instances, but I don't think it holds true this time. This is something different." She pressed her lips together in a tight line and looked down at the basket. "I need to be alone. If there's a vision for me, the quiet will help. Would you deliver the biscuits to the traders?"

"Yes, of course." Charlotte swallowed hard. "Is there anything else I can do to help?"

"Just be careful." She gestured at the ship on the horizon. "Please."

Lucia embraced her before turning back and hurrying off toward their cottage. Charlotte watched her go with a gnawing sense of unease. After a moment, she continued toward the dock alone. The weight of the basket grew heavier with each step she took.

Charlotte wondered what, if anything, her mother had already envisioned. She knew persecution had been a way of life for her ancestors for hundreds of years. But it had all been unwarranted. Witches called on no deity for their magic. Their talent was a gift they'd been born with. They hadn't asked for it. And when they practiced it, they took great care never to cause harm.

Keep the secret and harm no one. Those were the two rules they'd all been taught since before they learned to walk. If outsiders only knew the hearts of those they'd sought to persecute, perhaps they would have been kinder. Right away, Charlotte scoffed at the thought, knowing full well that witches' intentions didn't matter to those who wished to hurt them.

People had always feared what they didn't understand. Fear bred hatred. And hatred bred violence. Just as she knew the sun would rise in the morning, she knew people would destroy that which they could not comprehend.

She pressed on, trying to forget the ship that had failed to draw her concern prior to her conversation with her mother. In all likelihood, it was nothing. Just unnecessary worry from a queen who had lived through nightmares Charlotte could only imagine. Maybe there would be no vision. Maybe they could all just continue to live out their days in peace.

As she neared the dock, she came upon a group of children frolicking on the beach. They giggled as they ran about, oblivious to their queen's apprehension and unaware of the world beyond their isolated paradise. In the dunes, stationed like sentries, their contented mothers watched them play.

They were all so happy here, so carefree. Charlotte smiled at the children. They could be themselves in this small settlement, using and honing their skills with no risk of inciting an uproar among their neighbors. Charlotte took in the sight of the cozy cottages nestled in the grass just beyond the beach. Inside those homes, magic could be practiced freely, without fear of the swinging nooses or stake burnings favored by outsiders. She shuddered at the thought of those dark days of the past.

She pressed on toward the dock until a child named Anne came skipping on the sand behind her. "Hello, Princess Charlotte!"

The girl's younger sister, Lizzie, barreled toward them, desperate to catch up. "Wait for me!"

Charlotte bent down and tapped Anne's upturned nose with her finger. "There's no need to call me princess, little one."

Lizzie drew closer, running as fast as her little legs would carry her. She'd nearly caught up with her older sister when her bare foot hit a loose pocket of sand that gave way beneath her. She lurched forward as her legs shot out behind her, launching her head first into the tightly packed granules and shell fragments that lined the water's edge.

She landed with a hard thud. "Ouch!"

"Oh no!" Anne clasped her hand to her mouth. "Are you hurt?"

Spotting a trickle of blood on Lizzie's knee when the little girl rolled over, Charlotte dropped her basket and raced to her side.

Lizzie sat up, dazed. Glancing from her wounded knee to the disturbed sand around her, she spotted the offending shell right away. She plucked it from the sand and then chucked it straight into the ocean. "Stupid oysters!"

Charlotte smiled, happy to see Lizzie was well enough to be angry. "Oysters are good to eat but not very good for falling down on."

Beside her, Anne giggled.

Lizzie scowled at her sister. "Why didn't you wait for me?"

Anne shrugged. "I thought you would catch up."

Lizzie's expression twisted with fury as she held up her hand, palm forward, and aimed at Anne.

Charlotte's eyes grew wide. "Lizzie, no!"

But it was too late. A bright white light had already flashed in the little girl's palm and hurled forward until it smacked against Anne, who fell backward as soon as it struck her.

"Oof!" Anne groaned as she tried to sit up.

Charlotte gasped. In her childish anger, young Lizzie had forgotten to hide her magic and had left all of her power visible. Experienced witches knew better. They would have hidden it as a matter of course. But the little girl hadn't yet learned to control her emotions. It probably hadn't even occurred to her that she might be seen.

Immaturity combined with magic made for a terrible mix.

Charlotte glanced at the passing ship before she turned back to Lizzie. "What did your mother tell you about using your powers out here in the open, on the beach?" She gestured toward the ocean. "With passing ships that might see us?"

Lizzie lowered her head in shame. "To not."

"That's right." Charlotte reached down and helped the little girl up. Together they walked to where Anne sat in the sand, still wide-eyed and stunned. Lizzie remained quiet while Charlotte checked on her older sister. "Are you all right, Anne?"

When she nodded, Charlotte pulled the shaken girl to her feet. She placed little Lizzie's hand in Anne's and bowed forward, commanding their attention.

"Walk together. Take care of one another."

Both girls gave a solemn nod.

"And no more magic until you are safe in your home." Charlotte wagged her finger, just as her own mother had done when she'd misbehaved as a child. "Do you understand?"

"Yes, ma'am." Lizzie gave her a penitent look as she dusted the sand from her dress.

Charlotte watched them scurry off, hand in hand. On any other day, their behavior might have given her a good laugh. But not today. She squinted at the ship on the horizon, hoping with all her heart that there was no one aboard the vessel with a spyglass pointed her way.

Chapter two

Charlotte crouched on a low stool beside the grinding stones. Under strict orders from the queen not to use any magic at all as long as the unknown ship lurked off their coast, she'd had to tackle the chore of flour grinding the hard way—despite the fact that the surrounding brush kept her well out of sight of passing ships. She turned the heavy wheel by hand while the sharp pangs in her back mocked her fervent longing to pulverize the grains by the sheer force of her will.

She knew that she could keep her magic subtle and unnoticed, even *if* the men offshore could see her. But then again, there'd been plenty of witches throughout history who had thought that they'd exercised ample caution in their own efforts—only to wind up tied to a stake while their neighbors cheered their impending fiery demise.

Best not to risk it.

She'd had plenty of experience grinding flour using this traditional, far less enjoyable method. Her mother had made sure that she, along with all the other witches, knew how to handle everyday chores without using their magic—just in case they were ever in a situation in which they *couldn't* use their special talents.

Charlotte had often thought the practice was a colossal waste of time and effort, even though Lucia had always insisted that there was value in knowing how to do things the usual way. But now, with her mother's uneasiness so evident, she didn't know what to think. She rubbed the ache in her back and tossed another handful of wheat kernels into the hole atop the grinding stones.

Overhead, a seagull offered a forlorn screech, as if he too knew things would remain difficult until Lucia's trepidation abated. Charlotte wished her mother would have a vision already. Just one prophetic dream showing they'd all be safe and could return to their usual way of living. Even practicing mundane chores would be preferable to the anxious waiting she endured now.

Lucia had had a vision just that morning. But it wasn't the one Charlotte had hoped for. This one had revealed a massive school of mullet off the eastern side of their island, so the queen had sent the men and older boys to do their fishing there.

We know where the fish are, but we don't know whether or not we're truly safe here anymore. What good are visions if they don't tell you what you really need to know?

She turned the wheel with a long sigh. *Such tedious work.* But she would soon be finished and could go for her morning swim. Warmed by the summer sun, the water would be the perfect temperature. She looked forward to diving in and forgetting all about wheat kernels and merchant ships and visions that hadn't come when she wanted them to.

"Charlotte!" A familiar voice called from just out of view.

Jolted, she whipped her head toward the footpath to find her friend Hannah rounding the corner at a rapid clip. Her raven hair whipped behind her as she ran and her cheeks flushed red from the exertion.

Charlotte noticed her friend's furrowed brow right away. She hadn't seen Hannah express concern about much of anything before. She wasn't sure she'd even seen her run...not since their childhood days anyway.

Charlotte jumped to her feet just as Hannah arrived at the grinding stones. "What is it?"

Before Hannah could answer, another friend named Catherine—though she preferred to be called Cate—raced down the footpath and came to a breathless stop in front of the women.

Charlotte's gaze darted between the two. The distress etched on Hannah's face was multiplied tenfold in Cate's youthful features.

Hannah found her voice first. "The queen sent for us...the three of us."

Cate wrung her hands. "I was in the middle of helping my mother deliver Lucy's baby when I heard. We're to go to the beach at once."

"Why?" Charlotte asked as she reached back and yanked on the first apron string her hand found.

"I don't know." Cate gave an exaggerated shrug. "I only know she's acting peculiar."

Charlotte's mouth ran dry. "Didn't you hear her thoughts?"

As soon as she uttered the words, Charlotte realized she'd never asked that question before. Cate's unusual talent of mind reading had mattered little in their life on the island. There were no secrets here.

"No, Lucia blocked me as soon as my gift manifested. I can't read her thoughts." Cate gripped her hands even tighter.

"She sent Abigail away with the children." Hannah's strained expression betrayed her nervousness. "She told them to *hide*."

Charlotte's throat tightened, and she threw her apron to the ground. "Let's go." She raced forward, leading her friends down the footpath toward the shore.

Darting between a final set of dunes, they emerged onto the sandy stretch where the villagers usually spent most of their free time. She knew the men had all gone fishing on the other side of the island, so their absence came as no surprise. But she hadn't expected to find the beach so empty.

No children played. No women worked on their crafts. No one splashed in the water. It was so unlike any other day on the island, Charlotte could only come to one conclusion. *Mother has had her vision.*

Charlotte spotted Lucia, perched rigidly on a long piece of driftwood. Stark in her stillness, the queen stared straight out at the ocean. Her haunted expression sent an icy chill racing up Charlotte's spine.

"I wish we had more time to prepare…"

Charlotte could barely hear her. "What is it, Mother?" She hurried toward Lucia, flanked by her two friends.

The queen drew in a deep breath and rose to meet them. Her eyes were dark and somber, reflecting a grief Charlotte could not fathom.

Lucia raised her chin and cleared her throat. "The time has come. You are not children anymore. You are women. And now you need to trust that what I am going to do will be not only for you but for the survival of our kind."

Charlotte exchanged a confused glance with Hannah and Cate.

"There is not a moment to lose." The queen scanned the massive expanse of ocean churning in front of them. "They are coming. And when they leave, you three will be with them."

Charlotte followed her mother's gaze and saw nothing but choppy seawater and blue sky. Even the ship they'd spotted the day before had sailed out of view.

"They?" Hannah pushed away the strands of black hair that clung to the sweat on her face.

"The pirates." Lucia spoke with a measured calmness.

Cate's jaw dropped. "We will be *with* them?"

"It is the only way."

Charlotte couldn't believe it. "But, Mother, we are ready to fight!"

The queen shook her head. "No, we are not."

"Surely we can beat them with our magic," Hannah said, her arms crossed. "They are mere men."

"Yes, but to what end?" Lucia's tone never wavered. "There are far too many of them, and their behavior exceeds the ignorance-fueled violence our people have faced before."

Charlotte couldn't imagine anything worse than what had happened in Salem Village, or in England, or Ireland, or any of the other places her ancestors had once called home. But as she eyed the amethyst amulet her mother wore, she knew the queen possessed far more knowledge than she did—of the past *and* the future.

"Cruelty is a way of life for these pirates. If we fight, there *will* be bloodshed." Lucia's expression hardened, revealing nothing but absolute determination. And with that, Charlotte knew her mother had made her decision.

Cate acknowledged the inevitable with a defeated frown. "Then there is no other way…"

No. There isn't. Charlotte could see it in her mother's eyes and hear it in the rigid tone of her voice. The queen had already exhausted all the options, and this unthinkable arrangement was the path they must follow—the one course of action that offered them their best, and possibly their only, chance of survival.

But that truth didn't make it any easier to accept.

"I don't understand how this could happen. How do they know about us?" Charlotte pressed her lips together to keep them from trembling.

"I can only assume that someone on a passing ship saw something they shouldn't have." Lucia stared at the waves that broke along the shore. "Whatever the source, these men would not come if it were only a guess."

Remembering the spat between Anne and Lizzie, Charlotte stiffened. Had that one childish mistake sealed their fate?

"We were too careless here." Hannah hung her head.

Lucia gave a sad nod. "We were." She paused before meeting their gazes once more. "The pirate captain will not leave empty-handed. It's a matter of pride. He collects beautiful women just as he does any other treasure. You will go with him as a distraction, to keep him from seeking out the rest of the villagers."

Charlotte's heart sank as she looked across the landscape of her beloved home. She'd lived in this island community her entire life. She had little knowledge of what lay beyond it, save for the stories her mother and the other original settlers had shared about their days in Salem Village so long ago.

Nothing about their experiences offered her any hope.

If she went with these pirates, would she ever see her home again? What would become of her and her friends? Without the queen's gift of foresight, she could only trust that her mother had made the best decision she could under the circumstances.

Cate's lip quivered. "Why us?"

"Do not despair. You each possess qualities that are essential for the success of this endeavor." Lucia cupped Cate's cheek.

Whether the queen had meant that as a prophetic promise or mere encouragement, Charlotte did not know. She chose to hear the statement as a promise—because anything less involved consequences she could not entertain. Not now.

Though she lowered her hand, Lucia kept her focus on Cate. "Your unusual gift will ensure your safety in the new village. Listen in on the thoughts of those around you so you will know if anyone ever suspects our secret. You can warn Hannah and Charlotte if a threat arises."

Cate nodded and swiped a tear from her cheek.

Lucia stepped in front of Hannah. "Your resilience will see you through the hard times ahead, and your powerful magic will be a great asset in your new life."

New life? When the queen turned to her, Charlotte bit her lip to stifle a sob. This sounded like a goodbye.

"He will not want me." Lucia reached for Charlotte's hands. "You must go in my place and lead our people."

Barely able to contain the swell of sadness that threatened to consume her, Charlotte blinked back her tears. "What will happen to you?"

Lucia squeezed Charlotte's hands. "I will stand with you until the end."

Unable to bear the thought of what was to come, Charlotte directed her frantic gaze to the village and then across the dune grass. She felt the warmth of the white sand beneath her feet and the cool kiss of the ocean breeze on her skin. All of these things she'd taken for granted, and now, as they slipped away, she wanted nothing more than to cling to them.

And she would miss her mother most of all.

Without warning, Cate's voice pierced the air with a high-pitched shriek. "They're coming!"

Charlotte turned back the ocean. Sure enough, a large ship with tall black sails, accompanied by three smaller sloops, had appeared on the horizon.

"It is time." Lucia stood in silence for a moment, as if she too struggled to accept her own plan. "You will settle in a new village. I have seen it in my visions." She glanced back at the boats. "I do not know how you get there. I only know that you *will*."

Charlotte could hardly believe her ears. Settle in a new village? Surrounded by others who didn't share their gifts? Would they have to marry them? Bear their children too? A relentless pool of questions swirled in her mind. She wished she knew what her mother had seen in her vision because, in that moment, she couldn't begin to grasp why this drastic measure was a reasonable solution to their problem.

The only thing she knew for certain was that they'd have to hide their magic. Her mother had emphasized that rule since Charlotte's training had begun. It hadn't mattered much then. But it meant everything now.

"Can't we return here to our island?" Cate's voice cracked.

How could they exist among those who would see them dead if they knew the truth? That experiment had failed countless times throughout history.

But this time would be different. It had to be. The queen had seen it in her vision.

Lucia dipped her chin and kept her voice low as she answered Cate. "No, my dear, do not come back. It is clear now that we are too vulnerable here. I must evacuate the others and find another home among the colonists, but we'll stay near the ocean where our powers are the strongest. Like you, we will integrate into another community and hide in plain sight. We will have to separate, but it ensures us the greatest chance for our survival."

Charlotte had never thought she'd hear such words. Two different kingdoms, one led by her and the other led by her mother. It didn't make sense.

In a heartbeat, the queen's logic became clear. The realization hit hard—hard enough to knock the wind out of Charlotte. They were going back to the old way of life, to living among the others. To hiding and pretending.

And they needed two kingdoms in case one of them didn't make it.

With her entire world crumbling around her, she could only wish it was all a terrible dream. But she knew that when she woke up the next day—wherever she woke up—she'd know it had all been real.

She closed her eyes for a long moment. When she opened them, she saw her mother studying her with a sad smile.

"Daughter, as of today, *you* are the true queen. Your descendants will lead the future generations."

Dumbstruck, she watched her mother remove the amethyst necklace and then place it around Charlotte's neck. The amulet landed against her chest, surprising Charlotte with its weight. She reached up and touched it, soaking in the warmth that emanated from the powerful gem.

The warmth turned to heat—a fierce and powerful force that soared through Charlotte's whole body. Beginning in her chest, the sensation raced through her limbs, all the way through to the tips of her fingers and toes. Jolted, she wobbled, but her mother steadied her.

Charlotte gasped as a flurry of memories—none of them her own—flooded her mind. Thousands of years of history and magic, hardships and victories, became known to her. From the ancient times when her kind were revered to the murderous witch hunts that had scarred them forever, she could see it all as if she'd lived it herself.

Now she knew what the queens who had come before her had known and what each of them had felt during their reigns...

Love. All-encompassing love. Charlotte thought it must be as potent as a mother's devotion to her children. She looked at Hannah and Cate. They were *her* responsibility now. She would protect them. And she would start today.

Her life would be one of service and sacrifice. Lucia had imparted that fact since Charlotte was a little girl. But now she understood it deep in her soul.

She'd trained for this day her whole life. She would be the queen they needed.

She had to be.

Charlotte's heart thundered in her chest. Though she did not yet share her mother's courage, she knew they were equals now, and they had work to do.

Lucia gestured to the amulet. "Hide it."

Charlotte reached up and covered the amethyst with her hand. She inhaled deeply to concentrate on the task. When she exhaled, the pendant flickered. Its light escaped between her fingers as the amulet and its thick gold chain faded out of sight. But she could still feel its presence.

She had no doubt that she always would.

"Well done." Lucia gave Charlotte an approving nod and wrapped her arms around her.

Charlotte sunk into her mother's embrace, understanding fully now the sacrifice they both were about to make for the sake of their people.

Before she pulled away, Lucia whispered, "You *are* ready for this."

Together, along with Hannah and Cate, they watched the ships sail toward them. No longer dots on the horizon, the closer they came to shore, the clearer their details became. Charlotte noticed the imagery on the main ship's flag, and it chilled her blood—a ghastly emblem of a skeleton with horns, an hourglass in one hand and a spear in the other. Only one ship displayed that banner. She'd heard the traders' stories about it—and the monster who led its vile crew.

Blackbeard!

Having heard her thoughts, Cate gasped and shot a panicked glance her way.

More men than Charlotte could count scrambled about on the deck, each one bigger and dirtier than the next. Her stomach turned and her throat went dry.

She looked to her mother, who stood with her shoulders squared and her chin held high. Charlotte attempted to mirror her body language, feigning the courage she hoped she would one day have. For a moment, she wondered if her mother faked it too.

"Remember, no matter what happens, we cannot reveal our magic to them," Lucia said. "When they leave here today, they must believe that their information was false."

Hannah kept watch on the approaching ships, and Cate let out a sad whimper. Their time was almost up.

Lucia enveloped Charlotte once more. "Do not be afraid."

Charlotte tried not to tremble in her mother's arms. She closed her eyes and held on tightly, certain this would be the last time they'd ever hug.

She'd never been more afraid in her entire life.

Chapter Three

Charlotte stood with Hannah and Cate, watching the ominous ship drop anchor offshore. True to her word, Lucia waited alongside them. The wind blew, almost thunderous at times, and whipped their lightweight shifts against their legs. But no matter how loudly the wind howled, Charlotte could only hear the pounding of her own heartbeat.

The unwelcome visitors began to lower their dinghies into the ocean. Charlotte counted the men as they gathered their oars and pushed away from the large ship. Twenty-five of them, at the very least. There was no telling how many had stayed behind on the big ship or trailed behind in the three sloops. Hundreds, she guessed. Far more than the number of peaceful residents on the island.

Her mother had been right. It would have been impossible to overcome such forces without numerous casualties.

Now it's my duty to protect our people. Charlotte touched the space on her chest where the invisible amulet rested. Though she kept it hidden, its presence remained in the forefront of her mind.

As the pirates drew closer, Charlotte spied new details about them. Most of the men were in rags. Filthy from head to toe, their hair hung in greasy ropes over their faces. They grunted and growled like wild animals as they rowed toward the beach. She grimaced at the repulsive sight.

They made their final oar strokes and—much too soon for Charlotte's taste—reached the shallow water just off the beach. Several of the men jumped out at once to pull the rowboats out of the tide and onto the sand.

One pirate barked orders at the crew before he threw a boot-clad leg over the side of the boat and jumped onto the shore. Wearing a fine velvet jacket and a tricorn hat, he bore little resemblance to the others. Charlotte presumed he was their captain, Blackbeard.

She kept a close watch on him as he swaggered her way. Smoke curled in menacing wisps around his braided beard, creating a fiendish haze about his wild eyes. She could barely stand to look at him, but she forced herself to maintain her position—no matter how much she wanted to run from him.

He'd strapped two leather belts across his chest, each one loaded with three guns. With a cutlass on his right hip and a dagger on his left, he could commit any number of gruesome murders in any number of ways.

He strode forward with bone-chilling confidence. Charlotte could now see that the smoke hovering around his face came from slow-burning rope matches he'd tucked under his hat. Still, she found little comfort in the fact that the effect had been choreographed for their benefit.

Despite the fancy black ribbons he'd used to secure his braids, he looked like a living demon to Charlotte. Her fingers itched to use her magic to expel him from their peaceful world. But she knew better than to act on instinct. Instead, she remained silent and still, as did Hannah and Cate.

Charlotte stole a glance at Lucia and found her mother's expression devoid of the fear that gnawed at her now. Awed by the sight of immutable strength, she swallowed her growing panic and stood as tall as she could.

The imposing pirate closed in on them. "I see the witches wait for me," he called over his shoulder to his waiting crew. Turning back to the women, he eyed them with a lecherous grin. "So, you knew I was coming."

"There are no witches here." Lucia's expression relayed nothing more than complete stoicism. "We are a small fishing village, settled here decades ago."

Blackbeard regarded the modest cottages with curiosity. "Where are your men?"

Following her mother's example, Charlotte locked eyes with the pirate captain. "Fishing."

He contemplated this, stroking his beard in a display of shrewd consideration before twisting around to look at his men. "Surely if they possessed magic abilities, they would have stopped us by now."

His raggedy crew murmured in agreement, but Charlotte did not yet dare to believe her mother's ruse was working.

"But I am not yet convinced." Again, he snaked closer to the women and narrowed his black eyes to slits. "Witches are well-known for their cunning."

Charlotte raised her chin in defiance as his gaze scraped over her.

Leering at each woman as he sauntered by, he came to a stop in front of Lucia. "Do you know the true test of a witch?"

"I am familiar with the stories." Her voice held strong and true, lacking even the slightest hint of emotion.

"If I bound you to a chair and threw you into the ocean, would you sink to the bottom or float to the surface?" He angled his shoulders forward, challenging her.

Lucia did not flinch. "I would sink, just as surely as you would."

His next move happened in a heartbeat, taking Charlotte's breath away. One moment, Blackbeard stood there, nodding at Lucia with an odd appreciation, and the next, he'd unsheathed the dagger from his belt and lunged at her.

Cate clamped her hand over her mouth to stifle a scream while Hannah curled her hands into tight fists.

But Lucia did not resist as he pressed the sharp blade against her throat.

Charlotte mirrored her mother's fierce resolve, even as her knees wobbled in terror.

"If I cut you, will you bleed?" His tone had turned vicious. He emitted a low growl. A hungry growl.

"Of course." Lucia stared back at him, revealing no sign of distress.

"I'll see about that."

Blackbeard raised the dagger and drove the blade down toward Lucia's throat in one quick motion, stopping a mere hairsbreadth from her skin.

Unable to contain herself anymore, Cate wailed a shrill scream that soared over the sound of the crashing waves.

But Lucia did not cower. She stood tall, radiating conviction. Stunned by her mother's strength, Charlotte wondered if the queen had seen this moment in her vision. Did she already know she would survive this encounter? Or had she simply made her peace with an unavoidable fate?

Hannah jerked forward, as if she might jump at the vile pirate, but Charlotte gripped her arm to keep her still and to remind her of their ultimate goal. A single aggressive action on their part could launch them into a bloody battle, the very thing they were sacrificing themselves to avoid. She shot a warning glance at Hannah, who gave an almost imperceptible nod of understanding.

Charlotte returned her attention to her mother—the only one of them who knew the end results of these events. As long as Lucia remained calm, so would she.

She didn't know what frightened her the most—the pirates or the idea of her courage faltering. Her brave mother's blood flowed through her veins. Even if she could not feel it, she knew it was within her. She could only hope that would be enough to carry her through the nightmare they endured now.

"Claims of magic and witches…" The pirate captain scoffed. "There are no witches here."

The men behind him grumbled their disappointment, leading Charlotte to believe they must have been looking forward to a violent spectacle. She had no sympathy for their dismay.

Blackbeard stiffened, as if he shared the disappointment of his crew. But then his eyes crinkled with a playful look, and he began to drag the tip of his sharp dagger along the exposed skin beneath Lucia's neck. As he watched the thin line of blood trickle down onto her white dress, a bizarre, delighted grin spread across his face.

Charlotte gritted her teeth, struggling to stay in place, fighting her instinct to stop the monster. Through it all, Lucia didn't even wince. How could she stay so strong in the face of this abuse?

The answer bloomed in her mind the instant the question appeared. *She is saving us. All of us. That's what queens do.*

She hoped Cate had heard her thoughts. She would need the reminder just as much as Charlotte had.

"You are fortunate I chose not to pierce that heart of yours." The pirate's nostrils flared. "You possess no power to stop me. No power at all."

Blackbeard jammed his dagger back into its sheath before turning his attention to the younger women. Charlotte glared at him, defiant, even though her heart hammered with a terror that echoed in her soul.

He stopped in front of Cate but said nothing. He didn't have to. Charlotte could have seen the young woman's fearful shiver from a mile away.

With a smirk, he ogled Charlotte. He smelled of salt, rum, sweat, and fish—a hellish stench she was certain she'd never forget.

"Red hair." He helped himself to a tendril of her hair, twirling it around his finger. "I bet this one has a temper!"

His audience of crewmen guffawed at their leader's performance, and the sound twisted an angry knot in Charlotte's stomach. She wanted to choke the life out of the revolting lot. But she couldn't do that. For now, at least, she had to bury her true feelings and play her part in the charade that would somehow, someday, make her kind safe again. Sensing her mother's steady gaze on her, she forced herself to remain impassive, just as Lucia had moments earlier.

In an instant, Blackbeard grew bored with her lack of reaction and turned his beady eyes to Hannah. He stepped in front of her, sizing her up with more interest than he'd shown for the others. Seeing the hunger in his eyes, Charlotte fought back her overwhelming desire to slap him.

Hannah tightened her already balled fists until her knuckles blanched from the pressure. Charlotte wished her friend could hide her emotions better. The pirate had been toying with them all along, trying to achieve the reaction she gave him now.

He lifted a lock of Hannah's raven mane. "But you. You're the feistiest of them all, aren't you?"

She didn't make a sound, but the fire in her eyes spoke volumes.

Blackbeard's lecherous grin returned. He clutched Hannah's neck. "I shall take you first."

Charlotte watched her mother hang her head, and the knot that had formed in her stomach turned to nausea.

The pirate released Hannah and then whipped back to Lucia, who raised her chin once more. "Are they all your daughters?"

"I love them all."

Charlotte knew, without a doubt, that her mother's answer had been an honest one. She blinked back the hot tears that welled in her eyes. She couldn't cry now, no matter how much she wanted to stay with her mother.

"Then this will be a very sad day for you." He brightened with a fresh surge of hubris.

Lucia maintained her composure. "We have surrendered peacefully to you."

He nodded. "Indeed you have, and that is the only reason you are still alive." He called back to his men. "There is no magic here, but I do believe I have found three new wives."

Cate let out a helpless cry, and Charlotte reached for her hand, squeezing it to steady the younger girl. Cate trembled harder as laughter rumbled through the crew.

The pirate scanned the modest cottages that made up their village. He narrowed his eyes, as if he were considering raiding them all. But he seemed to dismiss the thought in an instant and instead focused on the women again.

"Will you walk with us?" Blackbeard arched his bushy eyebrow. "Or must my men drag you to the ship?"

Charlotte squared her shoulders and gripped Cate's hand tighter. "We will walk on our own."

"Very well then." He turned to his crew. "Leave the old one. I have no use for her."

When Blackbeard began to saunter back to the dinghies, Charlotte followed. He reeked of smug arrogance. As if he'd just conquered them. As if he'd accomplished something they hadn't already planned for him.

As the foul men flanked her, she peeked over her shoulder to see Lucia blow her a kiss. Two wet tracks of tears glistened on her mother's cheeks. Charlotte feared her heart might shatter in that moment. She raised her hand to return the gesture, but the crowd of men engulfed her, blocking her view.

The crew laughed at Charlotte and her friends, mocking them, and bared their rotten teeth as they prodded them down the beach. When the women reached the boats, they piled in amidst the fetid crew. Blackbeard kept a tight grip on Hannah and pulled her down to sit beside him.

Charlotte craned her neck to look around the men, to venture one more glimpse of her mother. She spotted her right away, walking to the water's edge. The sight brought both pain and comfort at once. Touching the hidden amulet on her chest, she reminded herself that no matter what befell them, she must stay strong. She would lead her people, just as her mother had.

The men pushed the boats off from the shore, and they set upon the ocean, rowing toward the quartet of waiting vessels—and an uncertain future.

Chapter four

When they reached the largest of the ships, the pirates ordered them to climb the rope and wood ladder that lead up to the deck. Held back by a crew member, Charlotte watched her friends ascend behind Blackbeard. Though Hannah's expression remained darkened with fury, she scaled the swaying ladder without incident. Poor Cate shivered and shuddered with each rung she grasped.

Keep going, Cate. You can do it.

The young mind reader peered down at Charlotte. Her chin trembled, but she pressed her lips together in a tight line before turning back to climb the final few wooden rungs.

Charlotte studied the massive ship while awaiting her turn. It appeared even more fearsome up close with its array of cannons, ready to spit fire, metal, and death on anything or anyone who dared to get too close. She looked away and turned to the sea, which, despite its unseen dangers and sharp-toothed predators, seemed a far safer place to be.

I'd rather take my chances with the sharks.

The crewman beside her grabbed her arm with a hard jerk and gestured to the ladder. "Come on now. Up ye go."

She obeyed, eager to reunite with Hannah and Cate. When she reached the railing, two pirates snaked their arms under hers and hoisted her onto the ship's deck. She stumbled and barreled forward, nearly slamming into Blackbeard himself.

"Watch yourself." He gripped her shoulder to steady her.

As soon as she found her bearings, she realized that she and her companions were surrounded by men. Far more than had come ashore on the island.

Pirates—this one missing a tooth, that one an ear—crowded around them. A gruesome face gawked at her with one good eye and one empty socket lined with rotten, festering flesh. The cool sea air did nothing to abate the stench of unwashed men that hung in a hot, heavy cloud around her.

"You're aboard the *Queen Anne's Revenge.*" Blackbeard made his announcement with pride, as if it might be received as good news to his hostages. "I assume you've heard of her."

She'd heard of it all right. But Charlotte shook her head, denying any knowledge of the vessel.

He cocked his head. "You must know who I am."

"I know nothing of you." Charlotte shrugged, telling the easiest lie she'd ever told. It might have been a subtle dig, but it brought her immense satisfaction to take a stab at his ego.

"I am Blackbeard." He narrowed his gaze. "You'll remember *my* name for the rest of your days. However many that may be."

Charlotte reflected his icy stare back at him—even though she couldn't shake the fear that her mother had placed far too much faith in her. She couldn't begin to imagine how she might get her friends away from Blackbeard and his loathsome crew.

She stood still and searched the crowded deck for Hannah and Cate. But she couldn't see either of them anymore. They'd been swallowed up in the sea of stinking pirates. It would be a whole lot easier to feign courage if she knew they were safe.

"The marriage ceremony!" Blackbeard extended his arms, addressing everyone. "Get on with it!"

A short man with straw-colored hair hurried forward, propelled through the impatient crowd of pirates with shoves and crude insults. He clutched a ragged, leather-bound book.

A marriage? Charlotte's breath caught in her throat.

Having received a discourteous prod from one of their hosts, Hannah stumbled out of the crowd of men. She clenched her fists so tight, Charlotte thought she might throw a punch at any moment. Cate teetered through a gap in the pirate horde, pale as a sun-bleached sand dollar.

The man with the straw-colored hair cracked open the book with a yawn, never once glancing down at its pages. "May the most holy Lord above bless this marriage forevermore. Amen." He snapped the book shut.

"Amen!" The men all raised their hats in celebration.

Charlotte gulped. So that was a pirate marriage ceremony. If she had blinked, she would have missed it.

Blackbeard gave a satisfied nod and stroked the ribbon-tied braids in his beard while he assessed the women once more. Charlotte's head swam at the thought of the inevitable next step—the wedding night.

From the way he leered at them, his black eyes lingering across every inch of their bodies, she knew it was on his mind too. "Leave the black-haired one and drop the other two in the hold for later." He shooed away Charlotte and Cate without another word.

Hannah. Charlotte's heart seized for her friend. "Wait!"

The rowdy crewmen silenced in an instant. Blackbeard scowled at her.

"Let her be. I'll go." Charlotte stole a desperate glance at Hannah. "Take me instead."

Blackbeard erupted with a deep throated laugh. "Don't worry, lass. You'll have your turn."

"But—"

"Enough." The pirate gripped the handle of his cutlass and gestured to her with a nod. "Drop this one in the hold before I silence her for good."

Charlotte touched the spot on her chest where the invisible amulet rested. She wanted to kill Blackbeard where he stood. She wanted to save her friends from this horrible fate. She wanted...anything but this.

Keep the secret and harm no one.

She slumped over. There was nothing she could do to help Hannah. They had no plan, no way out, and nowhere to go. A grimy hand clamped down on her arm and yanked her away from Blackbeard.

"Too bad we can't have some fun now." A toothless crewman with a gummy grin pressed in too close to Charlotte's neck and sniffed. "While they're still fresh!"

He wheezed out a laugh and grabbed for the braid that hung down her back. She swatted his hand away, but he laughed again, seemingly glad to have any attention from her.

"Belay that!" Blackbeard shouted from somewhere beyond the filthy throng. "We need to depart now. It's time to move on. Get to your stations!"

A muscular renegade sauntered from the crowd, grinning. "I'll have mine now, Cap'n!"

He grabbed Cate around the waist, pressing her against his body as he leaned in to plant a kiss on the terrified girl's cheek. She shrieked in revulsion and covered her face with her hands.

Charlotte couldn't take it. She couldn't just stand there and let this happen. She lurched forward, reaching for Cate, only to be wrenched back by the two crewmen who flanked her. They squeezed her arms tightly, proving to her that she had no chance of saving her friends.

The invisible amulet grew warm against her chest. The sensation served only as a reminder of the power she could not use to save her friends. There was nothing she could do that would go unnoticed on the crowded deck. Nothing that wouldn't trigger the very persecution she had to prevent at all costs.

Without taking his eyes off the young man who'd dare to challenge him, Blackbeard snickered. He clutched Cate's arm and pulled her close to his side. "Right then. I'll let you know when I'm done with her."

Cate's lip quivered as tears pooled in her eyes.

Without warning, Blackbeard drew a curved dragoon pistol from the strap across his chest and promptly delivered a bullet between the insolent lad's eyes.

A roar of laughter erupted from the crew. Cate wobbled on her feet, but Blackbeard's tight grip kept her from falling over.

Two crewmen leaped forward before the young man's body hit the deck. And, with a swift heave, they tossed him overboard without so much as a grunt from their exertion. Their movements were so well synchronized, it occurred to Charlotte that the grisly scene had likely played out many times before. Her blood turned to ice.

"He's shark food now. He'll be more useful to them than he was to us." Blackbeard returned his pistol to its holster and glared at his crew. "What are you all looking at? Hoist anchor!"

Most of the men jumped to work right away, leaving the three women standing—and shivering—on deck.

"Onward! Stocks are thin and we need to resupply!" Blackbeard extended his hand to Hannah, as if he expected her to join him unforced.

But when she turned her nose up at him, the pirate seized her by the arm and propelled her to a low door. His quarters, Charlotte presumed with a sinking feeling in her chest. Hannah, a woman full of so much spitfire and determination, hung her head and went without a fight.

Though her friend's expression remained unreadable underneath the cascade of dark hair that hid her features, Charlotte suspected that Hannah had come to the same conclusion she had.

This was a hopeless situation.

She wanted to say something to help Hannah. If nothing else, to let her know she wasn't alone. But Charlotte knew that wouldn't be enough. No words would ever be enough to make this tolerable. Not now. Not ever.

Thick, calloused fingers wrapped around Charlotte's wrist and pulled her across the deck while she scrambled her feet in a rush to keep them under her. The remaining assembled crewmen parted in front of them and opened a path to a yawning square hole that descended into the bowels of the ship. The man holding her arm gave her a hard shove, sending her plummeting down into the darkness.

She landed in a heap beside Cate. Dust billowed up around her, choking her, as pain screamed up her spine. Overhead, a crewman barked an obscenity and slammed the rickety hatch shut. She clambered to her knees and looked around. Her eyes were slow to adjust to the meager light, but after a moment, her dismal surroundings began to come into view. Mostly dusty crates.

Charlotte touched her invisible amulet, trying to take comfort in its power. She'd started this day as the queen's daughter, and now, she was the queen herself. But she didn't feel the least bit competent in her new role.

"I think you'll be a great queen," Cate responded to the unspoken thoughts with a shaky whisper as she crawled to a corner of the hold.

It seemed impossible to believe, especially now that Hannah was trapped in Blackbeard's quarters. She blinked back the hot tears that welled in her eyes. It was her duty to protect these women with everything she had.

And so far, she'd been a miserable failure at it.

"You tried to help her." Cate slumped against the wall and drew her knees up to her chest. "There was nothing more you could do..." Her voice cracked and she drew in a ragged breath.

"I know you're trying to help me feel better about this, but I don't think there's anything you can say to ease this ache in my heart."

"I know...I feel it too...it's just..." Cate pulled the hem of her shift down to cover her legs. "I can't help Hannah, so I thought maybe I could help you."

Seeing her young friend shudder, Charlotte knew that Cate battled the raw emotion that she endured herself. "We're not going to give up. Can you read her thoughts?"

"No." Cate shook her head. "She's too far away for me to hear."

Pressing her hand against her roiling stomach, Charlotte sat still for a long moment. Blackbeard had spoken. They'd all suffer the same fate eventually.

"Do you think your mother knew this would happen to Hannah?" Cate's face pinched with anguish. "To us?"

Charlotte had wondered about that herself. Her mother hadn't had much time to make plans. The vision had come late, too late to evacuate the island prior to the pirates' arrival. Maybe she'd only seen bits and pieces of the future she'd intended to set in motion. Maybe she'd had no idea of the perils the three witches would endure along the way. "I think she would have warned us if she had known."

"That's what I think too." Cate dropped her hands to the floor and stretched her legs out in front of her, but her shoulders remained drawn up tight.

Desperate to quell her agony for Hannah, Charlotte struggled to focus her thoughts on finding a way out. There had to be a way to save her friends from this nightmare. "We need a plan."

"Now that you have the amulet, do you have access to her vision? Can you see what will happen to us?" Cate swiped a tear from her cheek and sniffed. "It would be easier to make a plan if we knew what to expect."

Charlotte shook her head. "I can see so many things now—spells my ancestors used, some of their memories too—but there's nothing from her." As soon as the words crossed her lips, she realized the one thing that set her mother apart from the queens who had come before her. Lucia was still alive. If her theory was correct, she wouldn't see the vision that had delivered her, Hannah, and Cate to this horrific situation until...

She swallowed hard at the unbearable thought.

Charlotte shook her head in an attempt to push away the misery that threatened to overwhelm her. She couldn't think of her mother now. She couldn't even think of Hannah. They needed to get to safety, and it was up to her to figure out how.

Craning her neck, she peered through the lattice in the hatch above. She saw the sails flap taut, heaving the ship forward. Footsteps thudded overhead while the men shouted orders, boasts, and lewd insults at each other.

Even if she could get out of the hold unseen, she couldn't make it all the way to Hannah without being caught. She stared down at her hands, imagining herself blowing the hatch off its hinges and then marching straight to Blackbeard's quarters to rescue Hannah. She'd strike down anyone who got in her way. She wouldn't stop until her friends were safe.

But I can't do that here. She hung her head.

Water sloshed beneath the hull, heralding the ship's progress with a low, rhythmic whoosh. On any other day, in any other place, it might have been a soothing sound. But not now. Not when she knew they were sailing away from the only home she had ever known. And definitely not while Hannah was trapped with that vile beast.

A fresh surge of nausea struck and she squeezed her eyes shut. She'd give anything to have her friends safely back on the island. But with each lap of water against the hull, her mother, and the rest of her village, slipped farther and farther away. She exhaled a mournful sigh and leaned against a crate.

There had to be some way to escape from Blackbeard and his wretched crew without revealing that they were witches. She gripped the invisible amulet tighter, hoping for a vision, or a plan, or anything that might help her figure a way out. But nothing came to her.

Chapter Five

Charlotte sat in the grimy hold beneath the ship's deck, huddled with a trembling Cate amid crates, cannonballs, and ballast stones. The hot, damp air—thick with the stench of soured ale and the charcoal of gunpowder—enveloped them. Tapping her bare foot against the dusty floorboard, she struggled to concentrate on her primary responsibility—she needed to get Hannah and Cate to safety.

She had never endured anything like this before. She'd never been around *people* like this before. While the men on her island couldn't be described as the gentlest of souls, not one of them would have treated their female counterparts with the coarse cruelty the pirates had displayed.

Thinking of Hannah, her mouth ran dry. No man from her village would have ever behaved the way Blackbeard did. On her island, all were respected, all were equal. But that clearly wasn't the case here.

If this was the way of the outside world, she couldn't fathom how she could protect her friends in their new life. She'd already failed Hannah, and if she didn't come up with a plan soon, she'd fail Cate too.

I wish I could just take them back home.

For the thousandth time in the hour, she missed the wide expanses of beach on her island. The soft dune grass that tickled her feet, the powdery white sand, the pink sunsets, and the scent of fresh sea air. The way she, Cate, and Hannah had been carefree and safe. She cursed herself for taking it all for granted.

Above them, thin shafts of light streamed in through the lattice of the hatch, casting a meager glow on Cate's terror-stricken face. A couple of impatient pirates had already stopped to peer down at them with chilling grins. Since Cate could read the men's thoughts, Charlotte couldn't fathom what her young friend experienced each time those unwelcome visitors appeared. Her unusual gift had once been a blessing, but now it had surely become a curse.

Though it wasn't cold, Cate's teeth chattered. Charlotte held her tighter, wishing she could take away all the fear and horror that must be racing through the girl's head like it raced through hers.

"How will we get out of here?" Cate's voice quaked.

Charlotte stroked her hair. "I don't know."

The tears in Cate's eyes reminded Charlotte how inept she was at being queen, not at all like her mother. *She* would have provided a more comforting answer. "What I meant to say is that I'm still thinking. But trust me on this, we *will* get out of here."

Somehow.

Cate shivered again. Charlotte couldn't blame her. Though she was now the queen, she'd done nothing to earn the girl's trust. Or Hannah's. She doubted if she ever could, or whether she even deserved to after what had happened since their capture.

Charlotte refused to let her mind wander to a dark place. Her mother had chosen the three of them for this journey. And she wouldn't have done it if it wasn't in the best of interest of their people—all of their people.

"Remember all that my mother said about her vision. We're to settle in a new village." She gave Cate's hair another comforting stroke.

"She didn't say whether we'd settle in that village on our own…" Cate blanched with dread. "Or as Blackbeard's wives."

A horrifying thought. Charlotte hadn't considered that possibility, and she had nothing to offer in the way of a soothing response. Not an honest response at any rate. And there was no point in lying to a mind reader. She rose to her feet and began pacing, as if each step somehow brought her closer to a solution.

A moment later, they heard a whispering noise that had nothing to do with the waves lapping at the ship's hull. Charlotte jerked her head in the direction of the sound and spotted a whip-like tail disappearing into a dark corner.

Cate let out a high-pitched yelp.

"Rats." Putting on a brave front, Charlotte kept her voice as steady as she could. The pests were fitting company on a boat filled with men like Blackbeard.

"Oh, there's another one!" Cate pointed to a nearby ballast stone, where a pair of beady eyes stared back at them. She grabbed a discarded ax handle and began to flick it in the direction of the darkened corner to keep the hungry rodents away.

"How are we going to get out of here?" Armed with the ax handle, Cate rose to her feet. "I don't see how we can do it without using our magic."

"We have to keep our magic a secret. Even now." Charlotte continued her pacing. *Especially now.* She swallowed hard. *They've already thought us to be witches once. If those men see anything unusual or something that they can't easily explain, they'll blame us…and then they'll kill us.*

Deciding to take advantage of the daylight they had left and relieved she had something to keep her mind and hands busy, she began to peek in some of the open crates in search of anything they might be able to use to aid in their escape while Cate did her best to keep the rats at bay. With cautious optimism, she bit her lip and opened the first container.

Sugar.

She moved on to the next, lifting its lid in the hope of finding weapons or tools that could be used as weapons.

Cloth. Four bolts of it. No doubt ready to be fashioned into ridiculous, useless gowns.

She continued, opening each crate only to find more sugar, more cloth, and some dried leaves she didn't recognize. After what seemed like an eternity of searching, Charlotte hadn't come any closer to devising a way out.

Exhausted and frustrated, she slumped against a tall crate and wiped the sweat from her brow. Men clamored around on the deck above them—stomping, laughing, and yelling in a whirl of ceaseless activity. Charlotte gritted her teeth and began to pace again.

Hearing a familiar caw, she stopped mid-stride and shifted her gaze back to the hatch, where she could see bits of the blue sky through the lattice.

A bird with gray and white markings soared into view and then back out of sight in an instant. Had Charlotte glanced away for even the slightest second, she wouldn't have seen it. "There's a seagull!"

Cate swatted at an emboldened rat. "Seagulls always fly over the ocean."

"Yes. But only close to land." *Don't you see? We're not headed out to sea. We're running parallel to the coastline. Southward, I think.*

Cate wrinkled her brow and tilted her head.

The framework of a plan began to take shape in Charlotte's mind. It would have to involve a *bit* of magic. If they did it right, the pirates wouldn't guess that their captives had been responsible.

"I have an idea, but we should wait until Hannah is with us." It would take all three of them to manifest such a complicated undertaking. Even then, there were no guarantees they would be successful. And, if it all went horribly wrong, she wouldn't want Hannah in Blackbeard's presence for the aftermath.

She considered each step of her plan, giving her mind-reading companion the opportunity to hear it all.

Cate nodded after a moment, and a hopeful grin spread across her face. "Yes. I think that will work."

"It's not without risks. You understand that, don't you?"

Cate's smile faded. "Death would be preferable to this hellish waiting. I'll do whatever it takes to get off this ship." She jabbed the ax handle at another rat.

Charlotte continued to run the plan through her mind while they waited for Hannah to return. She tried to anticipate every possible complication. Any number of things could go awry. That much she knew for certain. Still, the more she thought about it, the more convinced she became that it was their only chance.

Moments later, a gruff voice boomed overhead. "Put this one in the hold with the others."

The hatch creaked open, bathing the space in a wash of sunlight before a dark form appeared and cast a long shadow over them.

Charlotte's eyes adjusted to the light, allowing her to see who stood above them—a man with a fuzzy mane stared down at her.

Another shadow appeared in the overhead opening. The new form that blocked the light was much smaller than the last. *Hannah.*

So many questions flittered in Charlotte's mind as her friend began to descend the ladder, shivering despite the unbearable heat. But she dared not ask them.

"She did not fight him." Cate kept her voice low, but it quaked nonetheless.

"How...how can I help her?"

With a tear in her eye, the young witch gave a somber shrug.

As soon as Hannah's feet touched the floor, she whirled toward Charlotte, her eyes black with rage and her fists squeezed tight.

Charlotte's chest seized in agony at the sight of her friend. In that moment, she wanted nothing more than to provide some measure of comfort, anything to ease the pain that Hannah had so carefully masked with anger. She opened her mouth to speak, only to close it again before uttering a single word. She had no idea how to help her friend.

Hannah snarled with fury. "I have obeyed our rules *this* time, but I cannot promise that I won't seek revenge against him."

"You may get your chance." Cate pointed to Charlotte. "She has a plan."

Hannah arched her eyebrow, but her voice remained bitter. "Oh? Does it involve me killing him?"

"No. I'm sorry." Charlotte shook her head, wishing she had a less disappointing answer for her. "But there is a way we can escape with our secret still intact."

Chapter Six

C harlotte studied the lattice hatch to make sure no crew-men were within view. Seeing no one, she whipped back to the others and began to lay out her plan.

She extended her arms and gestured for the women to come closer. "Join me."

Hannah and Cate each took hold of her hands, forming their magical circle, and they all closed their eyes. Charlotte's body buzzed with an almost unbearable combination of abject fear and fierce determination, but she drew in a deep breath to calm herself, the same way her mother had shown her so many times before.

Enveloped in a light only she and the others who shared her gift could see, she gripped her friends' hands. "One mind, one spirit, one focus."

The hidden amulet that hung from her neck made its presence known when it began to vibrate and grow warm. She relished the rush of the sensation. Her own magic whirled within her, amplified for the first time by the pendant.

Her power spread out, intermingling in an invisible tangle with the forces brought to bear by Hannah and Cate. Anyone who might have looked down into the hold would have seen three women, locked in a fervent prayer for their salvation. At least that's what Charlotte hoped they would presume. Any other assumption would warrant a death sentence.

The magic began to take hold, swirling from deep within her chest and radiating out to her fingers and toes. Pure and bold, it coursed through her body with immeasurable power and speed. She knew the others felt it too when Cate let out an awestruck gasp and Hannah's fingers quivered.

Charlotte set her sights deep under the ocean. In her mind's eye, she saw tiny, vaporous glimmers of force drip from the witches' pool of magic before plummeting through the thick hull of the ship, down to the ocean floor below. She envisioned the magic droplets they'd created spreading out, each one encasing a single grain of sand.

At first, just a few grains responded with only a slight tremble, but more and more began to move with them. Charlotte soon saw billions of particles start their ascent from the bottom of the ocean. They rose through the water, piling atop one another yet remaining just under the surface of the waves.

With the great swell of sand in position, the women let out an enormous exhalation in unison, blasting their unseen magic up through the hatch. Charlotte blinked her eyes open as sweat streamed from her forehead. She knew the last bit of their carefully disguised magic had slipped through the latticework above.

Suddenly propelled by the force of the wind their spell had manifested, the *Queen Anne's Revenge* lurched forward, causing Cate to stumble. The pirates on deck cried out in alarm.

Charlotte suspected that the crewmen had just spotted the enormous sandbar in the ship's path. She exchanged anticipatory glances with her companions.

They rushed to a corner of the hold and huddled together to brace themselves for impact while the men above them called to each other with panic-tinged shouts. The sandbar was too close, and it was already far too late to avoid it. The magical wind continued to propel the ship forward toward the imminent collision.

With a long scrape, followed by thunderous crackles of splintering wood, the *Queen Anne's Revenge* smashed onto the bar. Though they'd known the jolt was imminent, the women barely managed to keep their footing as the ship listed hard.

"It worked." Beaming, Cate clapped her hands together.

Charlotte understood her joy, but she hushed her right away. "They can't suspect that we caused this."

The vessel tilted even farther, losing its seaworthiness faster than Charlotte had expected. She grabbed her friends' hands to keep from falling. A second deafening crunch of cracking wood echoed from outside.

One of the accompanying sloops must have hit the sandbar as well. She smiled to herself, without the slightest sense of remorse.

Mayhem broke out on deck. Men bellowed and cursed as they ran back and forth, this way and that, in a chaotic effort to save their lives and their valuables. They pounded like an elephant stampede, rattling the wooden ceiling of the hold and showering the witches with dust, dirt, and sand. Charlotte ducked her head down to protect her eyes from the falling grit.

"Grab the gold! Get the loot into the longboat!" Blackbeard's voice boomed from above.

While Charlotte listened to the chaos she'd caused, she spotted a new threat on the opposite side of the hold. It seeped in slowly, first gathering in the lowest corner, but then it expanded across the floor at a rapid pace.

Seawater. Dark, frothing, and menacing, it advanced in silence, soaking everything in its path.

Charlotte's chest tightened, but she said nothing. Next to her, Cate was distracted, having already grown frantic listening to the pandemonium on deck. She didn't want to add to the girl's anxiety by calling attention to the rising water. Besides, she'd discover it on her own soon enough.

The incessant drumbeat of footsteps continued overhead as the men did everything they could to secure their material possessions and their escape. Though their shadows came and went, not a single man stopped to free them.

Charlotte's heart pounded harder. *The pirates will leave us to die here.* She turned to Hannah and saw no fear in her friend's expression. Only angry determination.

It didn't take long for the seawater to cross the slanted floor and reach them. Cate whimpered as it crept across her toes.

Shivering from the icy jolt, Charlotte huddled closer to the girl. "Don't worry. We have plenty of time."

Cate must have known that was a lie, but Charlotte couldn't allow terror to reign over the three of them. They had to keep cool heads if they were to have any chance of survival.

The rapidly rising water sidled up to her calves. Unseen things lapped at her ankles in its murky depths—seaweed, small fish, rat tails. She hoped the men above completed their evacuation before the ocean crawled up to their necks—or worse. She shook her head as if that might banish the unwanted thought.

It didn't.

Somewhere far off, she heard Blackbeard shout, "Get back, dogs! No room in this boat. You're on your own."

"Where are we supposed to go?" The man spoke with high-pitched desperation.

"Wherever you want." Blackbeard didn't hesitate to respond. "I release you from your duty."

Cate stared at Charlotte with eyes as wide as two moons. "Blackbeard's leaving!"

Not even honorable enough to help his own crew, the devil.

The water had climbed up to their waists by the time the noises on deck died away. They waited several more minutes to give the men ample opportunity to clear out. In that seemingly infinite stretch, the ocean continued to pound against the ship's hull.

Hannah stepped forward. "I think they're all gone now."

"Let's take a peek." Charlotte pushed through the dark swill to climb the ladder. Her wet linen shift clung to her legs as she climbed. With a hard push, she swung the hatch open and craned her neck to peer around the deck.

The pirate crew had deserted the ship. The only sounds she could hear came from the sea itself and the men who shouted at each other from quite a distance away.

"All clear!" She motioned for Hannah and Cate to follow her.

Cate gnawed on her lip. "But where did they go?"

"They've abandoned the ship. Which is what we must do as well." Thinking it was what her mother would have done, Charlotte kept her tone matter-of-fact.

"But how?" Cate wrapped her arms around herself. "Aren't they still out there?"

"I'm sure we can find a way to avoid them." Hannah had already begun trudging through the water to get to the ladder. "Regardless, we can't stay here. Come on."

They emerged, one by one, from the dismal hold and then struggled to maintain their balance on the sharp angle of the deck. Charlotte motioned for them to keep down while they crawled to the side of the ship. Nestling in beside a cannon that had been secured in place with a thick rope, she peered over the railing.

As she'd expected, one of the sloops had run aground on the sandbar beside the *Queen Anne's Revenge*. Searching for the other two vessels, she spotted one sailing away, propelled by crewmen who worked its numerous oars at a feverish pace. But the third sloop was nowhere in sight.

Whisking Blackbeard to safety, no doubt.

Dozens of frantic men floated and flailed in the water as they tried to make their way to a nearby stretch of sandy beach. From the look of them, Charlotte thought it unlikely that they'd all survive the swim. She watched one slip in total silence beneath the surface of the water, disappearing unnoticed by his fellow crewmen. While the sight didn't give her comfort, it didn't cause her any great pain either.

"There are pirates about, but they're too busy trying to save their own necks to fret much about us." *For the moment, at least.* She glanced at her friends, who remained crouched low.

"We must stay away from them," Hannah growled. "As far away as possible."

Charlotte agreed with that. But where else would they find refuge? She knew they couldn't stay on the sinking ship, and jumping into the ocean with dozens of pirates wouldn't do. She crawled across the deck to the high side of the creaking, listing vessel.

She spotted another island right away. From her distant vantage point, it appeared to be a cluster of green trees atop a smooth line of white sand. With no pirates in the sea between the sinking ship and that far off shore, it seemed too good to be true—though it was a much farther swim.

"None of the pirates are swimming in that direction. We'll be safe there." She turned to Hannah, who was busy wringing out the hem of her dress. After the ordeal her friend had been through, Charlotte didn't want to make assumptions. "Do you think you can make it?"

"Without a doubt." Hannah turned up a portion of the hem along the right side of her shift and then tied the section in a tight knot.

Charlotte couldn't be certain, but she thought she saw Hannah stuff a small item into the fold before tying it off. "What—"

"It's nothing." Hannah scowled and twisted away from her.

The *Queen Anne's Revenge* screeched with a sudden jolt, protesting the force of the tide against its unsteady position. Charlotte's feet slipped from beneath her. Scrambling to catch her footing, she grabbed the closest baluster to keep from sliding all the way across the deck and dropping into the pirate infested seawater on the other side of the boat. Just like her, Hannah and Cate gripped the railing as if their lives depended on it.

"There's no time to waste." Squeezing the baluster tight, Charlotte hoisted herself to her feet to get a better view of their escape route.

The sea had settled to a manageable calm. Having spent their entire lives on the water, the women were all strong swimmers. They could easily make it to the island. She just had to find a way to get them off the ship first.

Charlotte angled forward and spotted the massive sandbar beneath them. Too shallow to jump. Searching the deck, she sought out anything they could use to disembark. There wasn't much left on board—a spyglass, a discarded cup, a forgotten dagger. All useless. Finally, she saw a length of rope loosely coiled around the closest mast.

She snatched it up and tied it to the base of a cannon, tugging hard to make sure her knot would hold. She held out the end to her friends. "Who would like to go first?"

"I will." Hannah marched forward as if she couldn't wait to leave the ship. She grabbed the rope and climbed over the railing without another word.

Charlotte and Cate followed her. Once they had all gathered on the sandbar, they set off, swimming for the island in the distance.

The current stayed with them, and the calmness of the sea made for an easy, although lengthy, swim. Charlotte couldn't shake the looming fear that the surviving pirates might notice them, but she pressed on, drawing closer to the shore with each stroke.

At long last, the three of them crawled up onto the beach.

"Come along." Panting, she gestured for the others to follow her. "Let's go somewhere out of sight until they're all out of the water."

Their shifts, thoroughly soaked, now sagged under the additional burden of the sand they'd accumulated when they'd reached the beach, and their hair hung in wet, twisted tendrils around their faces. Charlotte dragged herself up behind a dune and knelt there. Hannah and Cate collapsed on either side of her.

She peeked through the long grass and gasped at the scene they'd just fled. The fearsome ship that had once wreaked havoc up and down the coast was now half-buried under the black sea with its masts poised at unnatural angles above the water.

Our handiwork.

The other stretch of land where Blackbeard's abandoned crew had fled was too far off for Charlotte to see exactly how many pirates remained. She could only make out their shadowy blurs in the distance. *Good.* With any luck, they wouldn't be able to see her either. Venturing a look up and down the shoreline, she confirmed that they were alone on the beach.

"I think we have escaped them." She exhaled with relief and threw her head back to stare up at the darkening sky.

They lay there in silence for a long time, bone-weary from the ordeal. So much had happened today. As much as Charlotte wanted to rejoice in the newfound freedom they'd achieved by escaping the pirates, she enjoyed no happiness. Now separated from their home and their families, they'd all lost too much—Hannah most of all. She bit down on her lip, barely able to stand the thought of it.

Uncertainty about their future wormed its way into her thoughts. There were so many questions to be answered now. Her mother had said they would need to join another settlement, to assimilate and hide in plain sight, all while keeping their secret safe. But where? What would they do next? Despite her exhaustion, Charlotte's head swam with worry for Hannah and Cate—and her ability to keep them safe.

Long after night fell, when the nearly full moon hung high in the sky, Charlotte peered over the dunes again to steal another glimpse at the remnants of the ships. The smaller sloop had already been consumed by the tide, but the flagship's main mast still stood tall, even as the ocean worked to claim the vessel.

She wondered how long it would take for the sea to swallow it whole.

Not soon enough. She glanced at the next dune, where her two companions had settled for the night. Gentle Cate, who had endured enough fear in one day to last many lifetimes, lay curled up in the soft sand. Her eyes were closed and her breaths came deep and even.

Charlotte hoped the girl enjoyed a dreamless sleep.

Beside Cate, Hannah sat upright with her knees pulled to her chest. Overwhelmed with guilt, Charlotte struggled to find words of comfort.

"I want to help. Just tell me what you need," she murmured in the quiet night. "Are you hurt? I could—"

"Not in a way that you can mend." Without looking Charlotte's way, Hannah lay down in the sand and closed her eyes.

Heaving a deep sigh, Charlotte slumped back against the sand dune, wishing for sleep to come swiftly.

As a child, she'd always assumed her happy, carefree days would last forever. And for a long time, they had. But those days were gone for good. Now, she knew what evil lurked in the world outside of her island paradise—the very evil her mother had worked so hard to protect her people from. She'd seen it firsthand.

And she knew she'd spend the rest of her life trying to protect Hannah and Cate from it.

Chapter seven

Charlotte woke just before dawn to the sound of the tide crashing on the shore. She looked about, blinking in the white glow of the sun as her eyes adjusted to the light. Tired and sore, she managed to sit up and shake the sand from her hair.

She spied Cate and Hannah, both still asleep, behind the dune they'd chosen as their refuge. Given all the two had endured, she decided to let them rest a while longer, even though Hannah stirred fitfully in her sleep.

The sand dunes wouldn't work for another night though. Charlotte rubbed the painful knot that had formed in her back. She'd slept no more than a few restless winks—all polluted with nightmares of Blackbeard emerging from a cloud of smoke, his hands poised to wrap around her neck. She'd woken with a start to every little sound—the wind, the waves, the scuffle of animals in the trees—always imagining his men had come to take them away.

She twisted around, staying low, to catch a glimpse of the water. The sea had grown rougher overnight. As the sun began to break over the horizon, streaking the sky pink, Charlotte noticed the fierce white caps breaking on the surface. How fortunate they'd been to make their escape yesterday, when the ocean had been calm.

The rising sun illuminated the hulking form of the *Queen Anne's Revenge*. The tide had gone out, revealing more of its hull, which came as a disappointment to Charlotte. Though she knew the ship enjoyed only a momentary reprieve, she would have much preferred to have seen it obliterated by now. She reminded herself that, in due course, the tide would rise again, the sandbar would shift, and the sea would continue its work of devouring the vessel. On its mainmast, the black banner with the drawing of a horned skeleton piercing a bloody heart still flapped in the wind, unaware that its demise would soon come.

Won't be long now. She shuddered at the memory of the previous day.

Beyond the sinking ship, Blackbeard's marooned crew slept on the shore of the island on the other side of the inlet. She could make out their shapes a little better in the daylight, but not by much. The stretch of water between their beach and hers would be much too far and probably too rough for most, perhaps any, of them to swim. From the looks of it, they were just as stranded as she was.

Rising to her feet, Charlotte shook the sand from her shift.

She had no sympathy for them. She had shown them mercy by running the ship aground near land, and that would be the extent of her kindness to them. It was a pity that Blackbeard had already secured his escape. She would have enjoyed seeing him stranded along with his crew—or succumbing to the sea and slipping beneath the water like so many of the others had.

Recalling the sight of the men struggling in the water, she considered how she had broken one of the most important rules. *Harm no one.* In her own defense, she hadn't known that anyone would drown as a result of her actions. But she hadn't known that they wouldn't either.

I did what I had to do.

Charlotte walked along the shoreline, studying the thick expanse of trees and wondering just what lay beyond them. She had not yet formed a plan to leave their island refuge, but she knew they couldn't stay here on this beach. It was just as vulnerable as the coastal home they'd left the previous day. They would have to take action soon if they were to survive, and as their queen, it was up to her to lead Hannah and Cate to safety.

She considered exploring the island with the hope that she might find a small village tucked away amid the trees or on a stretch of land within swimming distance. The alternative was to wait on the shore for a passing ship. But with that came the risk of encountering more pirates, and she didn't care for that possibility at all.

Inhaling the fresh sea air, Charlotte strode in the direction of the trees. She took a few hesitant steps into the unwelcoming maritime forest, wondering what she might find. Fresh water or fruit would be a good start. Anything to quench the thirst that burned her throat.

But all she found was an impenetrable tangle of roots, vines, and brush.

Disappointed, Charlotte retraced her steps and returned to the sandy beach to find that storm clouds had begun to roll in. She stifled a groan.

Hannah and Cate had both awakened in her absence and now walked along the shore to join her. Together, the three of them took in the view of the wrecked vessel.

"You are already a great queen." Cate gestured to the ship with both hands. "Look at what you did."

"What *we* did."

"It was *your* plan." Cate gave her an admiring grin. "And it worked beautifully. If not for your creative thinking, who knows where we'd be."

Hannah did not offer the same praise, and Charlotte couldn't blame her for her silence. So far, her experience under her new queen's rule had been a nightmare.

"I'm not certain we're much better off yet. I haven't seen a sign of life on this island. We need to find some sort of shelter. Food and water too." Charlotte tried to keep her tone matter-of-fact to keep her fear at bay. "It's likely to storm today, so the sooner we act, the better."

Hannah eyed the trees. "Have you found anything useful in there?"

Charlotte shook her head. "I only made it a few steps in."

First, they needed to walk the shore around the island to see if they could spot a settlement close by, or at least find some way to meet their basic needs. Charlotte's stomach growled as if to punctuate her thoughts.

Cate surveyed the opposite shore, where the pirates had begun to wake and move about. "What if some of them followed us here?

Hannah curled her lip into a snarl. "What if Blackbeard himself is hiding nearby?"

Unwilling to consider the implications of that possibility, Charlotte focused on the one known threat they had in that moment—the men on the other side of the inlet. From her vantage point, they were nothing more than dark, blurry figures in the distance. She couldn't make out their faces, nor could she tell if any of them looked her way. *Surely, we've been spotted by now.* She bit her lip, wondering if any of them suspected witchcraft as the cause of their current predicament.

Cate studied the stranded crew with the same intensity. Deep lines etched in her brow as though the effort required every bit of her concentration. "They're too far off for me to hear what they're thinking."

"Well, hello there!" The sudden boom of a male voice jolted the women.

At once, all three of them pivoted toward the unexpected sound. Charlotte's heart jammed in her throat when she saw a lone man walking their way.

Chapter eight

A pirate? Every muscle in Charlotte's body tensed. Her magic tingled at her fingertips, ready to do her bidding, as if that were an option she could utilize on the open expanse of beach. She curled her fists, trying to stifle the sensation. But the effort proved useless. Her magic couldn't be quelled any more than she could stop being a queen.

Hannah sucked in a sharp breath. Charlotte wanted to offer her promises of protection, but she knew those words would be meaningless now.

Cate remained calm as she kept her attention fixed on the approaching stranger. "There is nothing to fear. He means no harm. He's merely curious about us," she whispered. "And a little worried for our well-being since we appear to be wearing our bedclothes."

Charlotte fiddled with the thin material of her white shift. The simple dresses had been perfect back at home, but they wouldn't work in their new lives.

Despite Cate's assurances, Charlotte remained cautious. She raised her hand and offered the friendliest wave she could muster. "Hello."

As the man drew near, she could see his features with more clarity. His blue eyes reflected an air of kindness, and his fine waistcoat and breeches were nothing at all like the ragged attire of the pirates. With all those shiny gold buttons, he had to be of a higher social status and would likely possess better manners than the men they had just escaped from. Spotting youthful dimples upon his clean-shaven face, she thought he couldn't be much more than a few years older than she.

"Pardon me, misses, but it's not safe for you to be out here now. There's a slew of men from Blackbeard's ship just over there." He pointed to the shoreline on the other side of the inlet. "In fact, I'm here to confirm that none of them escaped to this island. Best to keep them confined to one area until they can be properly dealt with."

He furrowed his brow as he scanned the horizon.

He's keeping watch. The idea brought Charlotte an unexpected comfort, a sensation she dismissed almost as soon as it occurred to her. She still knew nothing about him. And she would not delegate her obligation to protect Hannah and Cate to any-one—no matter how kind he may seem.

"We have seen them, sir, but thank you for your warning." She pasted on a guarded smile. "Do you live here?"

"No. This island is uninhabited." He gave the three women a curious look. "Or, at least, I thought it was…"

His pause gave Charlotte the opportunity to explain their sit-uation, but she hadn't yet thought to make up the story of their past. And she didn't know if she should mention their time on the *Queen Anne's Revenge* at all. Feeling awkward, she bit her lip, leaving him to stew in his polite silence without her assistance.

The color rose in his cheeks. "I've come from Beaufort, just down the inlet from here. Word reached us that Blackbeard's flagship was sinking." He gave a curt nod toward the wreckage. "I see that rumor is true…though I've no doubt that the pirate captain escaped unharmed. He somehow always manages to stay out of our grasp."

"He's quite slippery." Cate commiserated with a nod. "He rushed away from the ship with no regard for his men."

"A shame, to be sure. But I can't say that I am surprised by his actions," the man said. "I take it you witnessed the wreck?"

"We were aboard the *Queen Anne's Revenge* when it ran aground." Hannah offered her reply without looking at him. Instead, she kept her steely gaze fixed on the stranded crew.

"I see." He let out a heavy sigh. "Probably not by choice, I would imagine."

Charlotte nodded. "That's correct."

"I wondered by your state of undress." His expression tightened with a mixture of sympathy and anger. "Did the pirate steal you from your beds? Were you taken from Charles Town? I hear he caused quite a stir down there—taking hostages and stealing everything he could get his hands on. Is that the way of it?"

That seemed as good of a story as any. Charlotte jumped in to answer before either of her companions could say otherwise. "Yes, that's exactly what happened. We're fortunate to have escaped. If it weren't for the run-in with that sandbar, we'd likely still be aboard his ship."

"I'm truly sorry to hear that." He frowned. "It must have been a very unpleasant ordeal for you three. If there is any way my crew or I can be of service to you, we shall be happy to provide assistance."

Moved by his concern, Charlotte relaxed, and the tension in her shoulders eased. "Thank you."

"And you're in luck. My merchant ship is scheduled to visit Charles Town just next month—a trip we've had to delay due to Blackbeard's activities in the area. We would be happy to return you to your home when we finally do set sail."

Hannah remained silent, but she drew her shoulders up so tight they nearly touched her ears. Charlotte knew the idea of boarding a vessel with yet another group of strange men didn't sit well with her. The thought turned her own stomach as well.

But they couldn't stay on this island forever.

"If you wish to accompany me to Beaufort, I'm positive we can find suitable accommodations for your stay in the meantime." With a sheepish grin, he ducked his head and then looked at Charlotte. "I apologize. I realize I haven't yet introduced myself. I'm Captain William Sutherland."

He removed his hat, revealing a mess of dark brown curls, and bowed low to the ground. Charlotte thought he looked humble and gallant all at once, a stark contrast to the men they'd just escaped.

Considering Cate's assurances, along with her own impression of the captain, Charlotte could think of no better way to get her friends to an established town. The only way off the island involved strangers and a boat. And she'd rather go with him than take her chances with the next person they encountered—whoever and whenever that may be.

"Thank you, Captain Sutherland." Charlotte smiled once more, though this time it was genuine. She introduced herself as well as her friends. "We'd be much obliged for your help."

He tucked his hat under his arm. "You must be tired and hungry. If you like, I can take you to my *Annabelle* now. She's quite old, but she's sturdy and has always met my needs."

Charlotte frowned. He wasn't the gentleman that he appeared to be. "Is this how the men of your town discuss their wives?" Making no effort to hide her disdain, she crossed her arms. "If that's the case, I don't think it's a place we want to visit." She'd already had more than her fill of disrespectful men.

The captain chuckled, but Charlotte failed to see the humor in the situation.

Cate covered her mouth in a half-hearted attempt to hide her amused grin. "I believe *Annabelle* is his ship."

Mortified, Charlotte felt the burn of a crimson blush rise in her cheeks.

"That's correct. I have no wife to speak poorly of. *Annabelle* is my merchant ship. Part of the family business." His eyes brightened, and he held up a finger. "In fact, I just brought back some new fashions from England on my last trip. There are still a few gowns left on board that we'd planned to deliver to Charles Town. It seems they could be put to good use right away though." He gestured to their linen shifts but kept his eyes above their shoulders. "You are most welcome to them."

His offer came as a relief to Charlotte. *Transportation and appropriate attire?* Perhaps her mother had known they would encounter Captain Sutherland in their travels. She stepped forward to speak not only for herself but also for her friends. "In that case, we gratefully accept."

The captain turned to lead them up the beach but stopped suddenly. "Forgive me, but I noticed you're missing your shoes as well. I'm afraid the walk is quite long."

Charlotte dug her toes in the sand. They didn't wear shoes at home, except on the coldest days of winter. But now, between her exposed feet and her simple dress, she felt shabby. Especially in the presence of Captain Sutherland and all his finery.

"I will bring my boat around this way so you won't have to walk as far." He propped his hat back on top of his head. "I wouldn't want you to risk injury."

Unable to help herself, Charlotte laughed. The men of their village wouldn't have behaved as Captain Sutherland did. In fact, they'd have been more likely to throw crushed shells in her path with the aim of getting a rise out of her. She wasn't used to being treated like a fragile sand dollar. "No need. We can manage the walk, I assure you."

The captain nodded and led them in the direction of his skiff, which he had left on the beach around a sharp bend. While they walked, he told them about Beaufort, which, despite its youth, had already grown prosperous through fishing, whaling, and trading. The only other town Charlotte had ever learned so much about was Salem Village. She hoped that this new settlement didn't share the same paranoia as its counterpart to the north. Slowing her pace, she dropped back behind Captain Sutherland and matched Cate's stride.

They walked side by side for several moments, and Charlotte kept a close eye on her young friend, watching for any change in her mood that would indicate that she'd detected a negative thought. But Cate's broad smile revealed a level of joy that seemed out of place given the events of the last day. Captain Sutherland's assistance was indeed a happy occasion, but she questioned whether it warranted the giddiness evident in the teenager's demeanor.

Finally, Cate whispered in her ear. "I think we're doing exactly what we're supposed to do." She paused, her eyes gleaming. "I think we're heading to the life Lucia envisioned for us."

Burdened with more caution than optimism, Charlotte raised a hand to the spot on her chest where the invisible amulet rested. Cate had no way to know that they were making the best choice by going with Captain Sutherland. She could only hope and wish that was the case. Which was all any of them could do.

Hannah marched forward with sheer determination chiseled on her features. Charlotte marveled at her strength. If her friend held onto any hopes and wishes about their chosen path, they remained buried beneath her clear desire to get far away from their captors.

Mulling over a multitude of speculations about the future, Charlotte remained silent as they rounded the narrow tip of the island and spotted the captain's small, flat bottomed boat on the beach ahead. She wanted to believe they were proceeding according to the grand plan they hadn't been privy to—that everything was as it should be—but she wouldn't allow herself to give in to those feelings. They'd endured too much to enjoy blind optimism. And she'd failed too hard in her first day as queen to have any confidence in her own competence.

Cate reached over and stroked her arm. A small, but comforting, gesture.

My thoughts haven't slowed since we left home. It must be maddening to hear it all.

Without hesitation, Cate offered her a compassionate smile.

They boarded the skiff and took their seats atop the thin slats of wood that ran across its midsection. Captain Sutherland pushed the boat from its perch on the shore and then jumped in to join them. He rowed swiftly, managing the feisty current with ease, and carried them to a much larger ship that waited in the deeper waters.

The crew aboard the *Annabelle* were decidedly more chivalrous than the beasts they'd encountered on the *Queen Anne's Revenge*. They greeted the women with respect before they even raised the anchor, and Charlotte didn't hear a single untoward comment from any of them. But it was Cate's jovial mood that convinced her that they might truly be safe on the ship.

After he doled out orders to his men, Captain Sutherland joined the three women at the railing. "I do think you'll enjoy your stay in Beaufort. It's quite lovely this time of year…though I doubt it will be as impressive as Charles Town. It is quite small in comparison."

Charlotte bit her lip, feeling a twinge of guilt for lying to the captain about where they'd come from. In the bigger scheme of things, she supposed, it had been a minor untruth. It wouldn't hurt anyone. And it helped her stay true to her mother's plans for them, which was, ultimately, all that really mattered. She was a queen now. She had to protect her people.

And there should be no guilt for fulfilling her most important duty. She'd have to get used to lying if she expected to survive among the outsiders.

"I'm certain it will be quite fine," she replied.

As they coasted through the inlet, Charlotte glimpsed the marooned pirates that dotted the sandy shore of the nearby island. She could see them more clearly from ship's location in the center of the inlet. The pirates were all awake now, and some of them turned to watch the *Annabelle* pass by. Hannah glared at them, but they couldn't have seen the hatred in her eyes from such a distance.

Cate gestured at the men. "What will happen to them?"

"If they're lucky, another pirate will come through here and take them aboard. Lord knows there's plenty of them in these waters." The captain studied the crewmen with narrowed eyes. "But our local militia will likely capture them before they have the chance for rescue."

"They can go to hell." Hannah curled her lip into a sneer. "The lot of them."

Everyone turned to her, eyes wide with shock. Charlotte bristled at the captain's stricken expression. He was probably unaccustomed to hearing a lady speak like that.

"We've had a very long and difficult journey, Captain." Charlotte tilted her head and spoke as sweetly as she could to make up for Hannah's harshness. "We'll be glad to finally have some respite."

After a quiet moment, the captain spoke again. "I have quarters available on the *Annabelle*. You are welcome to stay on board until your return to Charles Town. And you need not worry about these men." He gave a sweeping gesture to the crew who worked on the deck. "They won't bother you. I chose them all myself, and most of them have worked for me for years. You can be assured of your safety here."

"We appreciate your kindness, sir." Charlotte wondered, just for a second, if she should curtsy. She decided against it almost as soon as the thought popped into her mind. "We don't mean to be any trouble, but we're happy to stay on the *Annabelle*."

"Come to think of it, the quarters here are rather cramped." He tapped his finger against his chin. "My parents' house would be more suitable for you. There's plenty of room there."

Charlotte smiled at his thoughtfulness. "Thank you. That will do nicely."

"I believe I promised you new frocks. I shall go make those ready for you." He gave her a slight bow and hastened away.

As soon as he was out of earshot, Cate leaned in. "Oh my goodness, Charlotte. That man is positively silly about you."

Charlotte laced her hands together over the railing and lifted her chin. "What do I care about that?"

Cate gave a sheepish shrug. "He's terribly handsome. How could you *not* care?"

With a pang of envy for her young friend's joyful naivete, Charlotte heaved a deep sigh. Only Cate would fuss over romance at a time like this. What a luxury it must be to have no concerns in life other than finding a suitable husband.

"If you like him so much, then you may have him." She couldn't keep the bitterness from her voice.

"He's sweet on *you*." Cate pointed at her. "He might be a little stuffy, but he's a good man. Truly."

Charlotte dismissed her statement with a shake of her head. "We've only just met. He barely knows me."

Hannah, who'd been quiet and pensive since her outburst, pushed away from the railing and stomped off.

Cate hung her head. "It was thoughtless of me to carry on about these things in front of her."

"We must take care to be more sensitive. She's been through far more than we have." Charlotte tightened her jaw. "Besides, we have important work to do. There's no time for this type of foolish talk."

"Lucia did say you would lead the future generations though. That means marriage...and children." Cate's expression pinched with shame. "I—I thought I was being helpful."

Charlotte closed her eyes for a long moment. Her friend was right. Still, fussing over a possible suitor seemed like a selfish indulgence when her friends were suffering and there was so much work to do.

It just wasn't the right time. So, next month, when the *Annabelle* headed to Charles Town, Charlotte intended to gather her two subjects and go there to start their new lives. Even if that meant saying goodbye to the first decent person they'd met since leaving their home.

Those thoughts had barely settled in her mind when the *Annabelle* sailed through the narrowest portion of the inlet and the small fishing village of Beaufort came into view.

It was quite lovely, just as Captain Sutherland had said. She couldn't help but wonder if this little town was the new home her mother had envisioned for them after all.

Chapter nine

The *Annabelle* docked on the western end of the Beaufort waterfront. Bustling and beautiful, the town had many well-built homes and a variety of shops. From the deck of the ship, Charlotte could see that construction was already underway on even more structures. The village appeared poised for unfettered growth. At first sight, she thought it might be the perfect place to plant roots.

The captain had outfitted them in the fanciest gowns they'd ever seen, designed only for the wealthiest of women—women who didn't have daily chores to contend with. No, these dresses weren't for someone who might need to cast a fishing net or sweep a cottage floor. And they simply wouldn't do for anyone who would toil as Charlotte had at the grinding stones. They were costumes designed to project a specific image, and that's exactly how she intended to use them.

She drew in the deepest breath she could manage within the confines of her corset and scrutinized her gown's full skirt. Pretty but impractical. She fanned her neck, which had become sticky in the humidity. How anyone survived the summer heat in all these needless layers remained a mystery to her.

Pushing past her discomfort, she thought about the future of her coven. Could they settle here in Beaufort instead of fading into the crowds of Charles Town? As one of the crewmen lowered the gangplank down to the dock, Charlotte noticed a woman peering at her through a shop window with curiosity. Another resident, a fisherman, made no effort to hide his narrow-eyed suspicion when he looked her way.

A group of ladies, wearing dresses as fine as her own, gathered by one of the grand waterfront homes. She noticed their stolen glances and hurried whispers. None of them offered a welcoming smile or a cordial wave. No one looked at her with the kindness she'd hoped to find here.

The more Charlotte studied the town in which she considered building her coven, the more she doubted the choice.

Hannah and Cate settled in beside her at the railing while the crewmen finished their docking and disembarkation preparations. With so many outsiders around them, she couldn't ask Cate what thoughts she might have picked up on since their arrival. But she didn't need to. The youngest witch's furrowed brow confirmed Charlotte's own apprehension.

"Ladies." The captain approached them and gestured to the gangplank. "This way, please. I dare say the food we have aboard ship is substandard to what we can get you in town."

Charlotte hid her unease with a polite smile. "Thank you."

She led her friends down the gangplank, under the wary gaze of nearly every person on the waterfront. She thought again of the stories she'd heard of Salem Village. Had it all begun like this? With curiosity and suspicion?

And if they stayed at the home of the captain's parents, they'd be right in the thick of things. That wouldn't do. At least on the *Annabelle*, they were surrounding by people who'd been nice to them.

When her foot touched down onto the dock, Charlotte stopped—so short that Hannah and Cate almost collided into her. She turned back to the captain with a sheepish expression.

"Perhaps we would be better off staying aboard your ship? It seems as though we may not be welcome here."

The captain took in the sight of the gawking townspeople. "I apologize. You *will* be welcome here. It's just that you're the first strangers they've seen in a long while."

"I see." Charlotte's gaze darted to Cate, but the teenager offered no indication that she agreed with the captain's explanation.

"And, I hesitate to mention this, as I wouldn't want to frighten you..." Captain Sutherland lowered his voice. "There have been recent reports of witches living on one of the barrier islands. Given that, I reckon you can understand why they might be a little cautious of newcomers."

Cate confirmed his revelation with the slightest nod.

"Witches? Oh, dear." Charlotte gulped. "Well, I suppose one can never be too cautious."

"Precisely," the captain said with a sharp nod. "But fear not, I have no doubt that those stories are nothing more than just idle rumors. I'm far more concerned about the mermaids who've taken up residence in the inlet."

Studying his inscrutable expression, Charlotte couldn't decipher whether or not he was serious. She'd thought he must be an educated man, one unlikely to give credence to fanciful tales and magical creatures. Now, she wasn't so sure. Cate came to her rescue with a forced, but tinkling, giggle.

"Oh!" Charlotte laughed, hoping the relief she felt didn't show on her face.

"I know the residents will gladly accept you once they get acquainted with you," he added with a broad smile. "Just as I have."

Despite the captain's good humor, Charlotte still held reservations about entering the community. She turned back to her companions. Hannah's red-rimmed eyes conveyed her exhaustion. And Cate—who on any other day would have delighted in exploring a new village—gripped her hands tight, wringing them with obvious anxiety.

They've been through too much.

She met Captain Sutherland's confident gaze. "I think we will stay aboard your ship until that time."

Confusion flitted across his features, but he did not protest. "As you wish." With a sweep of his arm, he invited them to return to the *Annabelle*.

Cate released an audible sigh when she stepped back onto the ship's deck. Charlotte enjoyed the same sense of comfort in their relative safety, but she kept her expression impassive until the captain left them to go speak to one of his crewmen.

"Thank goodness." Cate kept her voice low. "Did you see how they stared at us? I thought they might march us straight to the gallows."

"This is not the place for us." Hannah scowled. "I think Charles Town will treat us better."

Charlotte considered this. Maybe Charles Town would be kinder to them. But she couldn't deny her strong pull to this place. Her mother hadn't promised it would be easy to find a new home for the coven. They'd be strangers no matter where they went. And fears of witchcraft almost certainly lingered throughout the colonies.

Longing for wise counsel, Charlotte touched the invisible amulet. She wished she could sit with her mother just one more time. For one more bit of advice. For one more embrace. She blinked, fighting back the sadness that swelled within her.

"Let's not rush to a decision just yet. We'll be here for a while. We might change our minds." She jerked her head toward the bustling town. "And theirs."

When the captain brought them below deck to show them their quarters, Charlotte realized he hadn't exaggerated when he'd said they were cramped spaces. The small, spare room housed thin berths better suited to children.

In here, the air clung to her like an extraneous layer on her frivolous gown—just like it had in the hold aboard the *Queen Anne's Revenge*. She glanced at Hannah, hoping there was nothing of this place that reminded her of Blackbeard's quarters.

Hannah flashed a tense half-smile. "I think this will be fine. At least this way, we know we'll all be together."

She gave Hannah's hand a quick squeeze before turning to Captain Sutherland. "Thank you. This is perfect."

He looked doubtful. "If you should reconsider, you are still welcome to join me at my parents' home. There's plenty of room for you there."

Charlotte couldn't deny her temptation to take him up on that offer. But even if she cast aside her qualms about the townspeople, the fact remained that she did not yet know where Blackbeard had absconded to. Nor did she know the fate of the stranded pirates. If they found their way to Beaufort as well…

She waved away his offer. "We'll be quite comfortable here."

"Well, I'll leave you to get settled in. But should you need anything, please let me or Barnes, the cook, know. He'll remain onboard with you, and he's a chap I trust with my life." He took a step toward the door.

Charlotte stepped forward, shaking her head. "We don't expect to be your guests, Captain. We intend to work for our room and board."

He stopped and lifted his eyebrows in surprise.

"Please don't feel like you must coddle us," she continued. "We're in your debt for saving us from that island."

"Ah, well, if you insist." He flashed an amused grin. "I'll tell Barnes he has some helpers. I might spend my time ashore, but a few of the men stay on board the ship when we're in port. It's no easy feat feeding their hungry mouths."

He held his hat over his heart and looked at her as if there was something more he wanted to say. But then he simply bowed and took his leave.

Chapter Ten

After a good night's rest, the women set to work. Right away, they slipped into the routine of preparing meals for the men. They helped clean the large vessel as well. Though Charlotte struggled with swabbing the deck in her uncomfortable gown, she didn't complain. Seeming just as grateful for a safe home, however temporary it may be, Hannah and Cate did not complain either.

By the end of the first day, several crewmen remarked that the *Annabelle* was the cleanest it had ever been. One even patted his bloated belly and announced that he'd never been so well fed.

The men were a congenial bunch. With the exception of their occasional compliments, they kept their distance—leaving Charlotte to wonder if the captain had ordered them to do so.

While she, Cate, and Hannah scrubbed the dishes from the evening meal, Barnes stepped into the galley. "Aye, there's a spark of life this old ship hasn't seen in a long time." His jovial voice boomed as he passed a pot to Cate. "We're glad to have you with us."

They all beamed at him, including Hannah. Charlotte's heart buoyed at the sight of her friend's smile. It had been the right choice to stay on board.

Once the galley sparkled from their efforts, they were able to relax for the rest of the evening. Hannah and Cate drifted back to their quarters, but Charlotte stayed on deck, where the cool sea breeze wafted in and reminded her of home. She stood at the railing, looking out over the dark water.

"It's late for you, is it not?"

She whirled around to see the captain striding her way.

"Oh." In an instant, she became aware of how she looked. The beautiful gown he'd provided for her was now stained from her day of cooking and cleaning, and when rebellious strands of her hair had escaped her braid hours earlier, she hadn't bothered to smooth them. She hated that she cared at all about her appearance when she had far more substantial issues to contend with. "And what brings you here? I thought you were staying on land."

"I came to see you." He slowed his pace. "I wanted to make sure you were comfortable here."

She tucked a renegade tendril of hair behind her ear. "Yes, we are. We slept well last night, and your crew has been very kind to us."

"You have everything you need?" He studied her with care.

Puzzled by the intensity of his expression, she cocked her head. "Is something wrong, Captain?"

"Forgive me." He stood straighter. "When I met the three of you and learned that you'd been taken by Blackbeard, I could only imagine what you might have endured. And I wouldn't be a gentleman if I didn't look after you all."

"I appreciate that." Charlotte held her head high. "But we three are stronger than we look."

"I don't doubt that at all. It's clear you have no need for me to dote on you. And yet you generously allow me to do it."

Captain Sutherland smiled. "I wouldn't have much of a purpose in life otherwise."

Playing along, she stifled a laugh. "Oh? Are there no damsels in distress in the lovely town of Beaufort?"

His smile faded and he moved to her side at the railing. "None so captivating as you."

Charlotte stifled a gasp. With her mission commanding her attention, she inched away from him and composed herself. "Have you heard any news of us among your townsfolk?"

Tilting his head, he raised an eyebrow. "Pardon?"

"The way they all looked at us when we arrived...I worry that they think poorly of us."

He turned his back to the rail and looked out over his town. Mirroring the motion, she did the same. With only a few oil lamps glowing in windows throughout the town, there was little to see in the dark of night.

"They've not mentioned anything untoward, though they have asked where you came from." He drew in a hesitant breath. "I've answered their questions honestly, so they do know you were taken from Charles Town."

"I see." Charlotte wondered if they believed him, but she decided not to ask.

"They bear no ill will for you, if that's your concern. These folks understand the dangers of piracy as well as anyone."

Relieved that he hadn't mentioned the rumors of witches again, Charlotte let out a sigh.

"After all, Blackbeard has a habit of slinking around here in Beaufort at times," he added.

Charlotte's knees wobbled and she gripped the railing to keep herself upright. "Is he here *now*?"

He shook his head. "I should think he'll lay low for a while after all the fuss from his latest criminal escapades." The captain eyed her with compassion. "And, you should know that he would not receive a warm reception from us. Our militia would welcome the opportunity to capture him now that our numbers have grown. He'd be a fool to come back here."

"The line between foolishness and arrogance is a thin one." Feeling sick to her stomach, Charlotte recalled the pirate's cocky swagger.

"Indeed it is. But let me worry about that beast." The captain held his chin high. "Don't give him another thought."

Such a strange thing to say. How could he possibly expect her not to worry about the man who had stolen her from her home?

The captain brightened, as if he were eager to change the subject. "There are plenty of productive, non-pirate citizens about who are quite excited to hear about your life in Charles Town." He held her gaze. "As am I."

Charles Town? What do I know of Charles Town? The grim realization took hold. *Nothing at all.* "We can discuss it another time…perhaps." She resisted the urge to fan herself, despite the fact that she felt terribly warm all of a sudden. "Not tonight though. I'm actually quite tired."

"All right then. I shall look forward to it." He tipped his hat in a most gallant fashion and bowed. "Good evening, Miss Charlotte."

There was something else she'd meant to ask him about. But whatever it was had slipped from her memory, leaving only a gnawing hint of its presence in her mind. She figured it would come back to her the next time she saw him—assuming she didn't get distracted by his charm again.

Though the night air blew cool and comfortable against her skin, it was only when she had gone below deck, away from him, that she was finally able to breathe.

chapter eleven

Charlotte watched the sky slowly brighten through the tiny porthole beside her bunk. Never before had daybreak filled her with so much dread. But after the night she'd had, dawn held no hope for her. It only heralded a passage of time she could ill afford.

"You're awake?" Cate's tired voice came from the bunk overhead.

Charlotte rolled onto her side. Pressing her elbow against the stiff berth, she propped her head on her hand. "Yes. Sorry if my thoughts disturbed you."

Hannah snored softly on the opposite side of the small cabin.

"It wasn't your thoughts," Cate said. "But your dreams. They were terrible. You and Hannah both had nightmares about Blackbeard. I managed to doze a bit in between them. But it feels like I've hardly slept at all."

With the wisdom that came with wearing the amulet, Charlotte had known for days exactly how to block Cate's unique magical gift. Encompassing her own mind with a simple wall of white, protective light would have kept her friend from hearing her thoughts. But without knowing what they might encounter in this new town, she'd kept the connection open, allowing Cate to answer her unspoken questions and letting the girl in on her numerous worries.

When Cate gasped with realization, Charlotte regretted that she'd given her unfettered access to her thoughts. By now, her friend would have figured out the truth of her nightmares.

"You...weren't...sleeping." Cate's voice quaked with panic. "Were you?"

There was no point in replying. Cate already knew. Charlotte sat up, steeling herself for the conversation she desperately wished she didn't have to have.

Hannah groaned and stirred in her bunk. "What's the matter?"

"I've had a vision." Charlotte struggled to keep her voice steady.

Cate shuffled overhead and slipped her slim legs over the side of the bunk. Jumping off, she landed on the wooden floor with a thud before taking a seat next to Charlotte.

"At first, I thought it was a dream too." Charlotte's heart thundered in her chest. "But it was too real. Too clear. There's no question in my mind that it was a vision—like the ones my mother had."

"What exactly did you see?" Hannah furrowed her brow.

"I was here...up on the deck. But it wasn't summertime. It was far too cool for that." She shivered as goose bumps rose on her skin. "But not so cold that I could see my breath. Autumn, I think...or maybe a mild winter day."

Hannah and Cate stared at her with rapt attention.

"I was watching the sunset when I heard his footsteps on the gangplank," Charlotte continued. "I spun around, expecting to find the captain, but it was..."

"Blackbeard," Cate whispered.

Hannah bolted upright, her complexion ashen.

"He didn't wear the burning matches in his hair, or even the gun belt, but he had his dagger and his cutlass." Charlotte wrapped her arms around herself. "He knew we were responsible for the shipwreck."

Cate's shoulders slumped. "You think some of the stranded crewmen told him that we escaped."

"Yes."

Hannah sucked in a sharp breath. "But the captain said the local militia would take care of them."

"Unless another pirate ship found them first." Charlotte corrected her. "I meant to inquire about their fate last night, but I forgot."

"Those men wouldn't go back to Blackbeard after he left them stranded like that." Hannah shook her head in disbelief.

Charlotte fiddled with the threadbare blanket on her bed. "Some wouldn't, maybe most. But it would only take one to spread the word of our escape."

"We obviously can't stay here." Hannah jumped to her feet and reached for her gown. "We should leave for Charles Town at the first opportunity."

"There's no guarantee he wouldn't find us there. Or in any other coastal town." Cate rested her hand atop Charlotte's. "We have time. Months, it seems, to figure out how to change the vision."

She was right. But with the specter of Blackbeard's return lurking in Charlotte's mind, months might as well be minutes.

Chapter twelve

The sun had already begun its descent for the evening, washing the horizon in red and orange hues. From her perch on the *Annabelle*'s deck, Charlotte studied the rippled surface of the water.

She needed information if she had any hope of protecting Hannah and Cate from Blackbeard. And while staying on the ship had provided temporary safety for all of them, they wouldn't learn anything new if they continued to keep to themselves.

Charlotte drummed her fingernails on the ship's wooden railing. Convinced that they should have a believable account of their past in order to safely venture off the *Annabelle* and interact with the townspeople, she'd struggled to come up with an acceptable story. It would have to be simple—one that they could all remember well. Not too many details, but enough to make it seem real.

She'd managed to dodge the captain's questions since their arrival. Where were their families from? How many brothers and sisters did she have? Who waited for her back at home? She must have stretched his patience to the limit by now.

It was all too much. Just as soon as she'd settle on a story that might work, she'd give it up. The thought of telling elaborate lies to everyone she met gnawed at her nerves. And the thought of giving an entirely false past to Captain Sutherland turned her stomach.

Deceit *had* to be part of her life now—it was the only way she, Hannah, and Cate would survive among the others. But she wanted to find a way to make it more tolerable somehow. She wanted to use a story that held more truth than lies. And she'd have to do it soon.

She heard the familiar thump of the captain's boot on the gangplank, and she whirled around to greet him. He had joined her for almost every sunset in the week since their arrival. Though she had protested at first—on the grounds that he needn't check on her—she couldn't deny that she enjoyed his company.

"Good evening, Miss Charlotte." He joined her at the railing. "It's another beautiful evening."

"Hmmm, it is." To hide her smile, she turned back to the shimmering water.

After several moments, Captain Sutherland broke their companionable silence. "People are beginning to grow curious… well, *more* curious about you." He paused. "I daresay I've whetted their appetite for news. The siege of Charles Town is all anyone ever talks about. They'd be glad to hear the account from an eyewitness."

Her heart quickened. "Ah, I'm afraid it's not as thrilling as one might think."

"Well, even so, I've spoken of you so often they're all dying to meet you. My family included." The color rose in his cheeks. "They keep asking when I'll bring you off the ship—as if I'm keeping you ladies captive here."

She sighed and glanced away from him. He'd been plying her to go out into the town for days.

"Charlotte…" He reached for her with the slightest gesture, as if he might take hold of her hand. But in an instant, he pulled back, seeming to think better of it. "You have nothing to fear here. I promise."

Oh, how she wished that were true. The rumors of island witches alone were enough to keep her from setting foot inside the town. But now she also knew that most of the stranded pirate crew had fled before the militia made it out to them. The captain had confirmed that fact himself a few nights earlier.

And no one had any knowledge of where those men had gone. Or whom they had gone with. For all she knew, they were all roaming around Beaufort, telling tales about captured witches who had used magic to sink their monstrous vessel.

The sun continued melting from the sky, spreading a warm orange glow across the cotton wool clouds. She stared at it for a moment, wishing she could share her troubles. "I know, Captain."

He sighed with mock aggravation. "How many times must I ask you to call me William?"

"I'm sorry…*William*." And she truly was—though it was for something altogether different. For all the lies she'd already told and was about to tell, "sorry" didn't begin to cover her remorse. He'd been so earnest, so truthful with her. Despite his stuffiness, as Cate had called it, she couldn't imagine there was a deceitful bone in his body.

"You must miss your family," he continued. "I can't say that I've spent much time in Charles Town, but I've heard good things. Whereabout is your home?"

Home. She wished she could tell him about her island and her life before Blackbeard. More than that, Charlotte wished she could tell him all about her mother. But those memories brought a pain she couldn't dwell on now. She drew in a deep breath to steady herself.

William had told her almost everything about his life already. He was the oldest of ten siblings. And he, along with his father and brothers, had built their family home themselves when they'd settled in Beaufort—a fact that clearly brought the captain great pride.

"Close to the waterfront." She gave him one of her usual vague answers and hoped the day would soon come when he'd finally stop asking for details about her past.

"That must be why you stand here looking over the water every night. Missing your home, I imagine?"

"Yes." She gripped the worn wood of the railing. "And I never tire of the sea air."

"Your family in Charles Town will be happy for your safe return." He frowned and turned his gaze to the water.

"No one waits for us." She lowered her head, wondering what he would think of that awful truth.

His eyebrows shot up in alarm. "No one? Surely someone misses you."

"Our family is gone." Another truth from her perspective. By now, her mother would have evacuated everyone from the island.

"The pirates...Blackbeard and his men..." He grimaced. "They did this?"

She laced her fingers in front of her to keep her hands from trembling. "That is why we cannot possibly tell the story the people of Beaufort want to hear. There is no exciting tale to tell...only heartbreak for us."

William sank back, his brow pinched with sympathy. "So, you are all three sisters?"

"Yes," she replied with a nod. They were sisters in spirit, if not by blood. That was a fib she could live with.

"Maybe some of your family survived. There's a chance—"

"No." She kept her voice flat, emotionless. "There is no chance."

She hated misleading him like this. But she could no longer avoid his inquiries, and the time had come to move forward.

He regarded her with a deep sadness in his eyes, almost as if he experienced her hurt with the same intensity she did. "Ah. Now I see why you've been so reluctant to tell me all you've been through. I am so very sorry."

She'd never known a man quite like him before. When he spoke those words of comfort, she could almost believe that he'd go to any lengths to make her happy. She pushed the thought out of her mind. She had too many responsibilities now to entertain those romantic notions. Perhaps Charles Town would be a better option for her coven. It would put some necessary distance between herself and the captain.

He rested an elbow on the railing. "Yet, you still wish to return to Charles Town. May I ask why?"

"It's where we belong." Charlotte clasped her hands together. "I just hope we don't cross paths with Blackbeard again."

"That criminal wouldn't want to encounter me." He squared his shoulders. "I'd show him no mercy."

Charlotte didn't doubt him. But she knew that if he dared to challenge Blackbeard, William wouldn't last long enough to fulfill that promise.

Chapter Thirteen

July 1718

As Charlotte dried the last of the washed pots in the ship's galley, she turned to Hannah and Cate. "I think I'd enjoy a walk this evening. Would you two like to come along?"

The women had taken to exploring the waterfront area in the weeks since their arrival in Beaufort. They filled their free time by popping into some of the shops or watching the fishermen unload their catches of the day.

Though Charlotte had braved those walks on her own a few times, she preferred to keep Cate by her side. The teenager's gift gave her a sense of comfort, and knowing the private thoughts of the townspeople had already proven most helpful. For all their initial misgivings about a barrier island populated with witches, no one still wondered if she and her companions might have come from there. Or, if they did, they hadn't thought about it in Cate's presence.

"I'll join you." Cate wiped her hands across her apron.

Hannah tossed a rag into a nearby bucket and yawned. "I think I'll retire early this evening. I'm quite tired today."

Charlotte watched Hannah amble by on her way out of the galley. Her raven hair accentuated the pallor that had developed since supper. "Shall I bring you some tea?"

"No." Hannah called back as she crossed the threshold. "I just need some sleep."

"I hope she hasn't caught a fever." Cate furrowed her brow as she whipped off her apron.

"Hopefully she'll feel better after a good rest." Charlotte had heard Hannah toss and turn and cry out in her sleep the night before.

"I should think so. Maybe tonight will be easier for her."

Unable to share her young friend's optimism, Charlotte didn't reply. Hannah's fitful sleep had become the norm, not the exception. And Charlotte had no idea how to help her. There were no spells to go back in time or to erase the horrible memories. Nothing at all to undo a madman's actions or a queen's failure.

Heaving a sigh, Charlotte gave the galley a quick check to confirm that they'd left it up to Barnes' standards before leading Cate down the gangplank and onto the dock.

The waterfront bustled with activity as the fishing boats returned to port for the day. Glancing across the road, she spotted signs of growth and blossoming prosperity everywhere she looked. Several new buildings had begun to take shape since their arrival, and hammers banged against wood throughout the town.

Without warning, a young man—Jasper, if Charlotte remembered correctly—leapt from the bow of a fishing boat and landed with a thud on the dock in front of them.

Startled, Cate jerked back.

But Cate shouldn't have been surprised at all. She would have heard his thoughts when he decided to hop off the boat. After a moment, Charlotte realized what her friend was up to.

She's just playing along.

"Pardon me, miss." Jasper grinned and tipped his hat. "Just have to tie the boat here." He held up a length of thick rope as if that explained his choice to jump down in front of them.

Charlotte stifled a giggle. It didn't take a mind reader to determine Jasper's intentions. And, from the look of it, he had accomplished his mission—Cate couldn't take her eyes off of him.

A rosy red blush bloomed on Cate's cheeks. "No harm done."

Don't get too attached to Jasper. Our scheduled "return" to Charles Town grows closer with each passing day.

Cate's expression darkened, but she said nothing. Instead, she waved goodbye to Jasper before continuing on her way. As they strolled down the waterfront, Charlotte spotted Captain Sutherland surveying a freshly cleared lot just across the road. She wondered what might become of the space. Another shop, she assumed.

The captain lit up when he saw her. "Hello!" He ran across the road to join them.

"How are you, Cap…I mean, William?" Charlotte smiled.

"Very well, thank you. In fact, I'm glad to see you both out and about." He peered over their shoulders, searching. "Is Miss Hannah around as well?"

Cate shook her head. "No, she's resting."

"Ah." William gave a quick nod. "I'd like to invite the three of you to a gathering at my family's home this Friday."

"A gathering?" Cate twirled toward Charlotte with bright-eyed delight. "That sounds fun!"

But Charlotte didn't think it was a good idea for them to attend. Taking great care to keep her plague of concerns from becoming evident in her expression, she bit down on her lip. What if they were asked about Blackbeard's siege on Charles Town? What if they were asked about their family? The less they intermingled with the locals, the better.

Best not to spend too much time with William either. Her chest tightened at the thought of leaving Beaufort—and him—to go to Charles Town.

"I'm really not sure..." Charlotte began.

"Please come." He held his hand over his heart. "My mother has invited the whole town, but it just won't be the same without you."

"The *whole* town?" Cate glanced down the dock at Jasper, who watched her with interest as he carried a fishing net to his boat.

The captain nodded. "Our numbers here are growing rapidly, so my mother wanted to do something to help foster a sense of community among the people."

But Charlotte had no plans to join their community. "Thank you very much for the invitation, but I—"

Cate gripped her arm, stopping her cold. "Will there be dancing?"

William grinned and kept his eyes on Charlotte as he answered. "Oh yes, there absolutely will be."

Oh dear. An unwanted warmth crept into Charlotte's cheeks.

Cate tugged on Charlotte's arm, pulling her attention away from the captain. One look at her friend's pleading gaze and Charlotte's resolve crumbled. "Please let your mother know that we're happy to attend."

Chapter fourteen

O n the following Friday evening, just as the sun began to set, Captain Sutherland arrived at the *Annabelle* to escort his guests to the party. Charlotte took in the sight of his polished boots and pale yellow waistcoat—one she hadn't seen him wear before. She thought it might have been made of a fine silk. It was all she could do to keep from swooning like a young girl.

Cate shot a knowing grin her way.

Queens don't swoon.

In an ineffective effort to hide her smirk, Cate lowered her head and dropped her gaze to the wooden floorboards beneath her.

Charlotte stifled a sigh. *It would be much easier to stick to the plan if he wasn't so…so…William.*

"I see you received the new dresses." He extended his arms, gesturing happily at all three of them.

Still trying to find her voice, Charlotte could only nod. They'd received their new taffeta gowns just a day earlier. As much as she wanted to hate them, she couldn't deny that they were beautiful.

"Oh, yes!" Cate twirled, sending the full skirt of her dress swishing about. "They're lovely!"

Hannah managed an appreciative smile. "Thank you very much."

Charlotte thought Hannah still looked tired, and a bit pale. She hoped the party wouldn't be too taxing for her. Hannah deserved the respite of an evening out more than any of them.

The captain extended his arm, inviting Charlotte to take hold. And she did—even though it sent her heart racing. They ambled down the gangplank and into the town together. Behind them, Hannah shushed Cate's giggles.

Unable to bear her own nervous silence any longer, she finally managed to draw in a reasonable breath. "Beaufort really is a lovely town."

"It hasn't been incorporated yet, but we're making progress. We already have the church and the market…and all the streets are laid out." He patted her hand, which still rested on his arm. "I see a great future for this place."

With a pang of regret, Charlotte nodded. His optimism wasn't without merit. She wished she could stay in Beaufort to watch it all come together. More than that, she wished she could stay with William.

Stealing an indulgent glimpse of his profile, she admonished herself instantly. *No. I cannot think of such things.*

She thought it strange that the little village held such a pull for her. Its grand homes and fussy societal norms bore no resemblance to her old life on the island. No woman here would ever be seen wearing a simple linen shift while tending, barefoot, to her daily chores.

The lifestyle differences hadn't been as intimidating as she'd expected. Different, yes. But not intolerable. As she strolled with the captain in her fancy dress and her new shoes, she realized she wasn't the same person who had left that island just a few weeks earlier. She had changed to meet the challenges of her new circumstances. Which, she thought, was exactly what a queen should do.

They crossed the rutted dirt road that ran the length of the waterfront, and the captain stopped at the cleared lot she'd seen him visiting earlier that week.

Charlotte pointed to the empty expanse. "What will this be?"

William waited a long moment before answering, as if he wanted to choose his words with care. "My new home."

"Right here on Front Street?" The view from the new house would be much like the one she enjoyed from the deck of the *Annabelle*.

"Yes." The captain nodded. "My thoughts of late have turned to the future, both for the town and for myself."

Cate emitted a faint, but gleeful, squeak, and for a moment, Charlotte envied her friend's unusual gift.

Charlotte blinked, resisting the urge to seek information from Cate. She couldn't entertain ideas about William's plans any more than she could reveal her magic. As queen, she needed to get Cate and Hannah settled in Charles Town, the place they'd claimed was their home—the place where Blackbeard would not find them on the *Annabelle* like she'd seen in her vision.

A group of townspeople passed by, dressed in their finest and chattering with excitement about the party. Charlotte stole a side glance at the captain and found him looking right at her.

"We should continue on." William stepped forward, leading them deeper into the town. "Wouldn't want to be late."

Charlotte didn't care if they were late or early or whether they attended the party at all. In that moment, she just wanted to be by his side—wherever that may be.

The Sutherland estate stood tall on the narrow street, a few blocks back from the waterfront. As they approached the stately home, Charlotte recalled all the stories William had shared about his family. She smiled, eager to meet them all.

The moment they entered the home, she felt as if she'd been transported to a different world. There were guests everywhere, with the women in colorful gowns and the men in their sharpest coats. Someone played a lively tune on a fiddle, and the mouthwatering scents of roasted pork and fresh baked breads filled the air.

A gray-haired woman rushed forward to greet them. She grasped both of Charlotte's hands and kissed her cheek. "You must be Charlotte!" She then extended the same greeting to the others. "Hannah and Cate!"

William brought his lips to Charlotte's ear. "My mother..."

Mrs. Sutherland whirled back to Charlotte. "I am simply delighted to have pulled you off of the ship for at least one night prior to your departure for Charles Town." She laced her arm through Charlotte's. "Let's see whom I can introduce you to."

It was a happy blur. She met many of the women, who were all just as warm and welcoming as Mrs. Sutherland. By the first hour, she'd accepted a request for Saturday lunch with William's eldest sister, Mary, and an invitation to the weekly quilting bee from his mother.

She began to feel quite foolish for ever doubting that they would fit in with the citizens of Beaufort. Nonetheless, she kept a close watch on her subjects. Hannah had drawn the attention of a few men, but she declined their invitations to dance. Cate, however, flirted with Jasper until he took her hand and led her to the dance floor.

Charlotte watched Hannah join a group of ladies who chatted in a corner. After a moment, she saw her friend laugh for the first time since their abduction. Heartened by the sight, Charlotte relaxed and glanced around the room in search of the captain.

He appeared before her, his hand outstretched, and bowed. "Would you care to dance?"

"I'm sorry." Suddenly overcome with self-consciousness, Charlotte shook her head. Heat bloomed in her cheeks. "I don't know the steps."

He waved away her doubts. "We're doing Ginny's Rant. It's quite new. My sister just made it up last Christmas. I doubt anyone knows it well...not even Ginny. You can just follow along while we all get it wrong together."

She laughed and accepted his hand. He led her to a large living room, where all the furniture had been cleared away and flickering candles lined the mantel above the hearth. A group of excited women stood shoulder to shoulder in the center of the room. He guided her to them and winked before taking his place among the men who stood in a line opposite the ladies.

The fiddler played and everyone began to move with the lively rhythm. For the briefest moment, Charlotte worried she wouldn't get the hang of the steps. But she soon realized—as they joined hands and twirled, changed partners, clapped, and shuffled through all the motions of the silly dance—that all of the guests in the room wore huge grins, whether or not they'd gotten the steps right. With her cares forgotten, she laughed right along with them while William twirled her toward the next fellow in line.

When the evening came to an end, the captain escorted the women back to the *Annabelle*. Charlotte couldn't help but notice the lightheartedness among the three of them, and she knew she'd made the right decision to attend the party.

When Cate and Hannah said their goodbyes and slipped below deck, Charlotte strolled to the railing. The captain followed her.

"I had a lovely time." She watched the moonlight dance on the dark water below. "I don't know why I waited so long to meet everyone."

"You may yet end up regretting it," he said with an ominous tone. "I saw my mother rope you into her quilting bee."

Charlotte raised an eyebrow. "Is that not good?"

"My mother's a bit strict about her stitches." He gave her a playful smile.

"Well, so am I. Stitches simply *must* be tiny." She laughed. "Hannah always complains that I'm too particular. I think your mother and I will get along famously."

Their laughter dissolved into silence, and she realized the joy in his mood had faded. Somber now, he had a faraway look in his eye. "The *Annabelle* sets sail in a week's time, Charlotte."

A hard lump formed in her throat. She didn't want to think of that, especially now after such a perfect evening. "That is a shame."

William gestured at the town with both arms spread wide. "You see that you are all welcome here. What will it take to get you to stay and make Beaufort your home?"

It was all she wanted right then, and perhaps forever. But forever wasn't an option. They'd have to leave before the weather turned cool—before Blackbeard found them. She'd have to consult with Hannah and Cate. Their comfort and safety would always be more important to her than her own happiness.

She opened her mouth to speak, but he stopped her. "You don't have to say anything right now. I know it's a lot to consider." He rested his hand on hers. "But I think you will find us a very pleasant lot. You've made quite a few friends this evening who don't want you to leave, and—"

"Yes, but—"

"*I* don't want you to leave." The corners of his eyes crinkled in a pained expression. "I don't know if that means anything to you, but I hope you will at least consider it."

It did. It frightened her how much everything he'd said meant to her.

He bowed low and kissed the back of her hand before taking his leave. As the sound of his boots retreated down the gangplank, she stared up at the stars and raised her hand to touch the hidden amulet that rested on her chest. Even though it remained invisible, she imagined the glow of its power, leading her to the place they were meant to settle.

But it didn't glow, or vibrate, or share any of its secrets with her. It offered no hints or visions to guide her decision-making. With a sigh, she realized that the queen's life was a lonely one.

Chapter Fifteen

Charlotte woke the next morning to see Hannah leap from her bed and rush out of their quarters with her hand clasped over her mouth. In the same instant, Cate hopped down from the top bunk.

Swinging her legs over the edge of her berth, Charlotte rose to go after Hannah. "Is she ill?"

Cate raised her hand, stopping Charlotte in her tracks. "I'm afraid it may be more than that."

The realization dawned on Charlotte before her young friend even finished the sentence. Given her experience helping her mother with midwifery, Cate would have suspected it even without reading Hannah's thoughts. "How long have you known...how long has *she* known?"

Have I been so wrapped up in being a good queen that I forgot to be a good friend?

"I've been concerned about her recent tiredness, but when she got sick for the first time yesterday morning...that's when I knew." Cate furrowed her brow. "Hannah didn't want to believe it. It was just now, when the latest wave of nausea struck, that she admitted to herself what it really was."

With a heavy heart, Charlotte stood frozen for a long moment.

And oh, if this is true, what will it mean for poor Hannah? A baby. Blackbeard's baby.

Charlotte dashed out of their quarters and found Hannah on the back deck, leaning over the railing. She had a distant look in her eyes, and her dark hair whipped in the wind. An unmistakable green tinge had colored her pale features. "Are you all right? Can I get you some peppermint tea?"

Hannah shifted away from her. "This? This is nothing."

Charlotte stroked her back. "You don't have to be brave right now. I'm here, and I will help you every step of the way."

"That's not what I mean...I...I dream of him. All the time." Her eyes flashed with panic. "I dream of him coming back."

"I won't let him get to you again." Charlotte shuddered as the vision of him aboard the *Annabelle* revisited her mind.

Hannah gagged and wretched over the railing once more. Wincing, she straightened up. "This is the fate I have earned."

"How can you say that? You don't deserve this." Charlotte shook her head. "*None* of this is your fault."

Hannah didn't reply. She only stared into the water.

"I'm going to get you that tea." Charlotte rushed off to the galley.

She returned with the steaming cup of peppermint tea to find Hannah standing with her back against the railing. Though the green tinge had faded, her skin remained pale.

"Here." Charlotte held the teacup out to her. "Try this. It will help settle your stomach."

"No...thank you." Hannah refused it with a flick of her hand. "I don't deserve any relief."

"That's not true at all!"

"Just leave me...please." Hannah sunk down to the deck and wrapped her arms around her knees.

Feeling helpless, Charlotte backed away from her and carried the tea down to their quarters. She met Cate's alarmed gaze as soon as she stepped into the room.

"Hannah won't let me help her." Charlotte gripped the tea-cup and paced back and forth in the small cabin. "There has to be something we can do."

Cate stayed quiet for a moment. "You know, sometimes expecting women are too sick to keep the peppermint tea down. So, my mother and I developed a way to give them the benefit of the tea without forcing them to drink it."

Charlotte halted her pacing.

"But it requires magic."

"Oh. Of course, it does." Charlotte slumped her shoulders.

"As long as we're quiet, no one will know," Cate continued. "This spell won't affect anyone but Hannah."

She wasn't wrong. Charlotte knew that. But she also knew that every witch who had ever burned at the stake or swung from a noose had thought they were being careful too.

She bit her lip as she thought of Hannah, sick and alone on the deck. Charlotte couldn't stand for to her friend suffer anymore. She hadn't been able to help Hannah before, but now she could. "All right. Let's do it."

"I can do it on my own, if you'd prefer."

"No. I want to help." Charlotte held her chin high.

Cate strode across the room and closed the door. "We'll just need one of her hairs."

Charlotte pulled a long, dark hair from Hannah's brush and dropped it into the peppermint tea before covering the cup with her hand.

Their voices a barely audible whisper, they began to chant in unison. "One mind, one spirit, one focus." Together they used their magic to vanquish Hannah's morning sickness with a simple, but effective, spell.

"It is done." Cate pulled her away from the cup.

Charlotte nodded. "It is done."

Chapter Sixteen

L ater that day, the three women worked to complete their chores. They polished the brass bell and swept the deck while they reminisced about the party. Hannah's healthy, natural glow had already returned, and the sun had given her cheeks a pink hue.

Charlotte let her gaze drift to the town. Could she even consider staying here now that Hannah's circumstances had changed so dramatically?

Cate stopped sweeping and answered Charlotte's unspoken thought. "I'd like to stay too. Not just because of Jasper either. I truly like this place."

Hannah froze, rag in hand, just as she was about to wipe the last of the salt spray from the bell. "You want to stay here? In Beaufort?"

Charlotte clasped her hands, nervous to begin this discussion with Hannah. "I've been meaning to discuss it with you actually."

She'd been thinking about it all day. Though she knew they'd likely have to leave at the end of the summer to avoid Blackbeard, she held out hope that their fate would change somehow. It was nothing more than a feeling—a strange gut instinct that told her to stay for now, even if it defied logic.

"I think we'll fit in nicely here, for rest of the summer anyway. There's still a chance that something will change and we can stay even longer," Charlotte continued.

"You mean *you'll* fit in." Hannah frowned. "I will always be the mother of Blackbeard's bastard child…how can I possibly have a life here?"

"No one needs to know that—"

"*I'll* know." Hannah pivoted away from her. "They say he has a home near here. What if he learns of the baby?" She twisted the cleaning rag in her hands. "He comes for me every night in my dreams."

"Do you think you'd be safer elsewhere?" Cate raised her eyebrows.

Hannah did not answer.

Charlotte touched the hidden amulet on her chest and longed for a solution. "Charles Town was not safe from Blackbeard. You know what happened there."

"Then I will travel inland." Hannah crossed her arms.

Charlotte couldn't believe her ears. Was she speaking of leaving them? Going off on her own without the protection of her coven? "You can't do that. I won't allow it!"

Hannah threw the rag on the deck. "I wouldn't expect you to understand."

The remark landed as hard as a slap. "I am your queen now. My duty is to you and Cate, and to the future generation. I will not leave a single one of you behind. Wherever we go, we will go together." Charlotte stepped closer to Hannah. "And you must remember, Blackbeard is not our *only* worry."

"Witch hunts." Cate grimaced.

"That's right," Charlotte said. "We've been accepted by this community. We can't be so sure that would happen elsewhere—especially with rumors circulating about an island full of witches."

"I see the way the captain cares for you. You may be welcome here, but how will I be?" Hannah hung her head. "I am pregnant without a husband...and no desire for one."

She wrapped her arm around Hannah's shoulder. "You'll be welcomed here just as much as I am. We'll tell them you were widowed in the Charles Town siege. They need not know more than that."

After a long moment, Hannah's expression softened. "I think that might work."

Cate clapped her hands together. "I had a feeling from the start that we would make this town our home."

"I did too. But still, we can't get too comfortable yet." Charlotte drew in a deep breath. "We know Blackbeard is out there somewhere...and we know he will come for us."

Chapter seventeen

In the quiet moments before sunset, Charlotte rested against the ship's railing, enjoying the welcome sense of relief that came from having made the decision to stay in Beaufort. She looked out over the community that would be her new home and reveled in the hopeful future that played out in her mind. Daring to imagine a life without Blackbeard, she saw the town growing, her coven right along with it. More homes and shops would spring up. The fishing industry would flourish. And the next generation of her kind would thrive here.

This is just what Mother wanted for us.

She clasped her hand over the invisible amulet—a simple gesture, but one that always reminded her of her mother. *Oh, how I miss you!*

The memory of their final embrace appeared in her mind unbidden. Her eyes filled with tears, but she blinked them away as fast as she could. She had to stay strong for the others. After all, Hannah and Cate had stayed strong for her.

They'd been selected to leave their families behind just as she had. Though they all shared that same loss, they hadn't spoken of their sacrifice. She smiled, just a little, marveling at their strength and her mother's wisdom in choosing them for this difficult journey.

They would do well here, among the citizens of Beaufort. Still, she couldn't help but wonder what had become of the rest of their island village. Had they found their way to a town like this one? Were Anne and little Lizzie happy in their new home? Charlotte hoped so. And hope was all she could do because if her mother's prophecy held true, she would never see any of them again.

"Maybe someday you'll tell me where you go with those far-away thoughts of yours." The captain stepped from the gang-plank onto the deck.

Charlotte straightened, jolted from her ruminations. "Oh, William…I didn't see you come up."

He smiled as he approached her. "I know."

"I have some news." Excited to share her decision with him, she felt the warmth rise in her cheeks. "My sisters and I have decided that we do not wish to return to Charles Town after all. We'd rather stay here."

The captain beamed with delight. "What brought about this change of plans?"

"Cate claims that your mother's party was the most fun she's ever had. And now I have all these social engagements that I must keep." She counted them off on her fingers. "There's lunch with your sister, and the quilting bee—"

Amused, he cocked his head. "So…social engagements were the tipping point for you."

Charlotte glanced away, certain she had turned an unflattering shade of red. "Yes, among other things."

"Other things?" He scrunched his face with intense curiosity. "What sort of other things?"

"Oysters," Charlotte blurted out.

With a playful glint in his eye, William gave a deep nod of understanding, as if any sort of shellfish might be a perfectly reasonable explanation for her change of heart.

"Yes, I believe they're the best we've ever had—especially the way your mother prepares them. And then there's your sister's strawberry pie. Also quite delicious. You must thank her for sending that to us." Running out of ways to dodge the true intent of his questions, she shuffled her feet. "And, of course, there's the people."

"The people are quite kind here."

"They really are. They didn't pester us for information about the Charles Town siege as I'd feared they might. They just accepted us." She forced herself to meet his steady gaze, knowing her next statement would be the one he'd been waiting to hear. "And then there's you. I have enjoyed our talks."

He dipped his head without breaking eye contact with her. "I have enjoyed your company as well."

They both rested their arms on the railing and looked out over the water. As much as Charlotte relished the peaceful quiet of the summer evening, she realized she needed to tell him of the latest change in their circumstances.

"There's something else you should know…" She hesitated to continue with the difficult news. "Hannah is expecting a child."

His expression darkened. "I presume her…*husband*…was killed in the Charles Town siege?"

Charlotte knew from his reaction that he'd already guessed the truth of Hannah's pregnancy. She nodded, relieved she wouldn't have to lie to him about it.

"Then I shall tell my mother and sisters about the young widow's plight." He gave her hand a reassuring pat. "Word will spread quickly; it always does. And I know the community will be glad to help her."

Charlotte thought of their quick acceptance in the town and wondered if the captain himself had facilitated that process in the same manner he intended to help Hannah. She resisted the urge to ask him. Whatever he knew—or thought he knew—about the women aboard his ship, he'd kept to himself. She saw no need to unsettle that balance now.

"Thank you." The words seemed wholly insufficient to express the full scope of her gratitude, but she could say nothing more on the matter. "We understand that you still need to tend to your business in Charles Town as scheduled. So, I think we should find lodging on land before the *Annabelle* sails again. The rough seas might be difficult for Hannah to manage in her condition."

"I think I will stay in Beaufort as well."

"Oh, no," Charlotte protested. "You mustn't let our plans disrupt your business."

"The *Annabelle* can make her delivery without me. My brother can take my place. I have pressing matters to tend to here in town." He studied her with an intensity she hadn't seen from him before.

"What pressing matters?"

"A rather interesting woman. She's a bit of a mystery, but one I'd never tire of trying to solve." The captain took both of her hands in his. "She is smart and beautiful. I daresay she captured my heart the moment I met her."

Charlotte drew in a sharp breath.

"I'll tell you a secret." His voice lilted with admiration. "I simply didn't think it was possible for someone to have such an effect on me...until I met you."

Her heart soared from those tender words. She searched for something to say, a secret of her own to share. But she couldn't divulge any of those—no matter how much she wanted to open up to him. She'd carry those to her grave.

He might not know everything about her, but he knew her heart and still cared for her. That was all that mattered. As long as she kept her true identity hidden, it wouldn't become an issue for them.

Her stomach knotted suddenly as realization struck.

Magic wouldn't be the issue that would divide them. Only one force could drive them apart now.

Blackbeard.

Chapter eighteen

The three women left the *Annabelle* and moved into the Sutherland estate, where they shared one of the many bedrooms in the expansive house. Though Charlotte missed her view of the harbor, she didn't mind the luxury of a soft bed made up with crisp, clean linens.

Mrs. Sutherland had welcomed them with open arms. Right away, Charlotte had informed her that she, Hannah, and Cate would be happy to earn their keep, just as they had aboard the *Annabelle*. But the captain's mother had heard nothing of it. "We have plenty of servants," she'd said with a hearty laugh. "We don't need three more."

After several days of reading, needlework, and idle conversation, Hannah paced the floor of their room. "There must be a pot I can wash or some water I can fetch from the well."

They'd all had a difficult time adjusting to a life of leisure, but at least Charlotte and Cate had been able to enjoy a bit of freedom during their time at the estate. They'd strolled the gardens at will and had even entered the kitchen on more than one occasion to bake special treats for the family.

But Hannah didn't enjoy the same freedom as they did. "They treat me like a prized pig!" She propped her hands on her hips and scowled. "They only want to fatten me up."

Charlotte stifled her amused grin. William had already informed his family of the pregnancy before they moved in. By the time Hannah had arrived at the Sutherland estate, his mother and sisters were waiting to swoop in and act as her guardians. The expecting mother was not allowed to exert herself unnecessarily—not on their watch.

The Sutherland women had a very different approach to pregnancy than what Charlotte, Hannah, and Cate were accustomed to. Back on the island, expectant mothers would continue with their daily chores right up until the pains of labor began.

"It is a bit unusual, but it won't hurt the baby if you spend your time relaxing." Cate ran a silver-plated brush through her hair. "Maybe you should try to enjoy the rest. At least you don't have to grind your own grain."

The mere thought of the flour mill brought an achy twinge to Charlotte's back. As much as she missed their island, she didn't miss that horrid chore.

"Let's go for a walk around town." Charlotte raised a conspiratorial eyebrow at Hannah. "We'll smuggle you out if we have to."

Cate giggled as she took a final stroke with her hairbrush and then placed it on the vanity. "Yes! It'll be good for all of us."

Hannah required no convincing. She bolted for the door before Charlotte even managed to stand up.

They made it all the way out of the house and into town without anyone stopping them to question why Hannah was on her feet. Feeling every bit of the muggy late summer heat, Charlotte slowed her pace while they strolled to the open-air waterfront market.

As she fanned herself, she kept a close eye on everyone around them. Moving off of the *Annabelle* and into the Sutherland house had likely prevented her vision of Blackbeard from coming true. But that didn't mean he wouldn't return to Beaufort. Even without a new vision to replace the first, she had no doubt he'd come for them—especially if he believed they were responsible for wrecking the *Queen Anne's Revenge*. Only now, she didn't know where or when it would happen.

Her mother's visions had been detailed enough that she could make life-altering decisions with confidence based on what she'd seen. But Charlotte had viewed only the slightest glimpse of the future. Hardly enough to make reasonable plans or have any confidence in her decisions.

When Cate touched her arm, they exchanged a worried glance, but neither spoke of Charlotte's concerns as they reached the open-air market.

Charlotte stopped and pretended to admire a display of embroidered kerchiefs while Cate eyed material for a new dress— as if she needed another one. Hannah strode forward to the next stall and peered into a basket of shell beads.

Stealing a sweeping view across the waterfront, Charlotte caught sight of a black tricorn hat bobbing above the crowd on the docks. Her muscles tensed, and she strained her neck for a better view of the man who wore it.

Cate followed her gaze. "He's not tall enough."

She was right. Charlotte caught sight of the man's shaggy blond hair and knew, for certain, that it wasn't Blackbeard. Still, her heart pounded as she continued to search the crowd.

"If he's here, he won't be able to sneak up on us. I'm listening for him," Cate said.

Far too often, Charlotte had thought of her young friend as someone to protect. It had become easy to forget that she could help.

Cate picked up a swath of indigo fabric and sighed. "Shopping would be much more fun…if only we had a penny to our names."

Charlotte nodded her agreement. They hadn't a coin to speak of between the three of them. But, in truth, she hadn't wanted for anything. William and his family had met all their needs and then some. "If we required it, the captain would—"

"Oh, he would, would he?" A picture of mock nonchalance, Cate set the fabric on the table. "Do you think you'll be receiving a proposal soon?"

Charlotte's heart soared at the thought. "I am quite fond of William." She studied her young friend's expression with care. "But I should think you'd know his intentions better than I would."

"I suppose I would, wouldn't I?" Cate gave her a mischievous grin before skipping off toward the next seller's stall.

With a few quick strides, Charlotte caught up to her.

Cate shook her head. "I'm not saying anything more on the subject."

"And I'm not asking you to." Charlotte smiled, catching sight of a familiar face on the dock. "In fact, if you put my business out of your head for a moment, you might notice that boy looking your way."

"Boy?" Cate spotted Jasper standing beside his boat. "He's no boy. He's older than I am."

"Not by much." Charlotte picked up a pretty piece of crockery that she had no use for.

"He's handsome, don't you think?" Cate waved to Jasper and then feigned fascination over the plate Charlotte held.

"In a rugged sort of way." She cared far less about his appearance than she did his treatment of her young subject. "Is he good to you?"

Cate looked at her with an unmistakable seriousness in her eyes. "Always."

That was enough for Charlotte. Cate's unusual gift afforded her the opportunity to know a man's integrity in an instant. She placed the plate on the table and looked for other interesting items to explore.

Hannah stayed well ahead of them, as if she preferred to be alone. While she looked over a selection of jars at one of the stands, she slipped a protective hand over her still small belly.

The gesture made Charlotte smile and gave her a bit of hope. "She's doing better, I think."

"Well, she's not sick anymore." Cate flipped a basket over, examining the weave on its bottom. "But she is far from all right. Didn't you hear her cry out in her sleep last night?"

"No." Charlotte cast a worried look in Hannah's direction as guilt swept over her. She'd come in late the night before, after watching William and the other men play ninepins. Drink and conversation had flowed freely, and she'd enjoyed spending the extra time with the captain. As soon as she collapsed in her bed, she'd drifted into the deepest of sleeps. She hadn't heard a peep from Hannah.

"Her nightmares of Blackbeard continue." Cate spoke in a hushed whisper. "Only now, she sees him coming to take her baby."

Charlotte's heart sank. "How awful!"

She wondered what she could do to help Hannah as they walked past more stands. Lost in her worries for her friend, she paid no mind to the wares that were on display all around her.

Cate ran her hand across another piece of fabric without looking at it. "I tried to reassure her—"

"I can't imagine there's anything that would reassure her now. Not as long as he lives." Charlotte gritted her teeth.

"If he comes here, don't you think the captain and all the other brave men of Beaufort would defend the town against the likes of him?" Cate asked.

Charlotte kept quiet. If her own mother had opted to sacrifice her child in order to avoid conflict with Blackbeard's men, then there was no hope for the little town—no matter how brave or strong its residents were.

Cate slumped. "I didn't think of that."

"It's all right." She stroked her young friend's arm. "We'll just have to stay vigilant. I'll do whatever it takes to keep you two safe."

Hannah suddenly rushed toward them, her face as pale as the moon. "Let's go."

Cate and Charlotte hustled to keep up with her, following her out of the market and back down the street before she finally stopped to speak to them.

"He's not far from here!" Hannah's eyes were wild and wide. "I heard some of the fishermen talking…"

Charlotte's mouth ran dry. She didn't have to ask who the "he" was.

"The governor has given him a pardon." Hannah spat those words as if they disgusted her. "He can roam as freely as he wishes." She wrapped both of her arms across her belly.

Charlotte's sense of duty burned in her veins. There had to be a way to stop Blackbeard from coming to Beaufort.

Chapter nineteen

September 1718

As summer gave way to fall, Hannah's belly began to grow, and word of her fictional husband's fate continued to spread throughout Beaufort. The townspeople showered her in sympathetic glances and comforting pats instead of the judgmental glares Charlotte had feared they would have doled out had they known the truth.

But Hannah didn't seem to appreciate their sympathy or care about fitting in anymore. The further she progressed into her pregnancy, the more removed she became.

Carrying a cup of tea, Charlotte joined her on the back porch and watched her for a moment as she practiced her embroidery—in sullen silence, as usual.

"I brought this for you." She placed the cup on the table beside Hannah. "But if there's anything else you'd like, I'm happy to fetch it for you."

Hannah acknowledged her with an absentminded nod.

Charlotte wondered, as she had so many times since their abduction, if Hannah blamed her for all that had happened. They all knew it was a queen's duty to keep her coven safe, and she had failed Hannah in that regard. Their lifelong friendship had disintegrated since their arrival in Beaufort, and she missed the simple times they had enjoyed back on the island. More than that, she missed the companionship of her friend.

They'd grown up together—playing, swimming, and talking about boys. Those days were long gone, and their lives were more complicated now, especially Hannah's. She knew that. But Charlotte believed they could manage the challenges ahead together. She only needed to repair her relationship with her old friend. They'd both be better for it. If nothing else, it would provide her with a way to assist Hannah. Even if that only came in the form of being a shoulder to lean on, she'd be grateful for the opportunity.

"Please let me help you." Charlotte took a ponderous step closer. "There must be something I can do."

Hannah locked eyes with her. "You think I will feel better if I talk to you about what happened, but I won't. I don't want to think of it at all."

"We don't have to talk about anything you don't want to. I just want to be here for you. I want to be your friend again." Charlotte took the seat next to her. "I miss you."

"I am still here." She pushed her needle through the linen, wincing as she stuck her finger.

"I think you know what I mean."

Hannah remained quiet for a long moment before her expression softened. "Cate says you've been worried that I blame you."

A hard lump formed in Charlotte's throat. Unable to speak, she only nodded.

"I don't. I never did." Hannah continued with her stitches.

With a swell of relief, Charlotte rested her hand over her heart. But the sensation receded almost as quickly as it had come when the guilt she'd heaped upon herself returned, unabated by her dear friend's absolution. She forced a smile in an effort to keep her pain from showing.

Hannah raised her chin. "There is only one person to blame, and I cannot do anything about him."

Neither can I.

New rumors of Blackbeard's whereabouts had been swirling throughout the town for weeks. He'd been spotted in the Carolinas and Virginia. One report even placed him in the Caribbean. He seemed to be everywhere and nowhere at once. Charlotte only knew two things for certain—the weather would soon become cool, and they had no way to stop him from coming to Beaufort.

And that meant she'd have to find a new home for her coven.

Charlotte said no more on the matter. She and Hannah sat together in comfortable silence, and, as the quiet moments ticked by, the tension in Hannah's shoulders seemed to ease.

"Why don't you tell me something to take my mind off of this boring needlepoint." She turned up the corners of her lips in an almost playful grin. "How about the captain? Is there any news?"

Charlotte sank back in her chair. *William.* He'd been so busy overseeing construction on his fancy new home; she barely saw him anymore. If it weren't for the fact that she'd occasionally delivered his lunch to the lot, she might not have seen him at all during the last few weeks. "I'm afraid there's no news to report with regard to him."

Hannah rested her embroidery on her lap and cocked her head.

Charlotte shrugged. "We haven't even shared a kiss yet. He's so…reserved; I doubt we ever will."

"And yet, he's building a house fit for a queen." Hannah arched an eyebrow.

"Oh! Do you think..." Charlotte gasped. "Do you think he's building that house for *me*?"

With a knowing smirk, Hannah raised the teacup to her lips.

A sudden breeze blew a gust of cool air across the porch, reminding Charlotte that the summer months had passed, that her days in Beaufort were numbered, and that her time with William might soon come to an end.

Chapter twenty

October 1718

Charlotte fanned herself with her free hand as she carried William's lunch to the construction lot. So far, autumn had been unseasonably warm, which had proven both a blessing and curse. Any day—any moment—the weather could turn. She knew that just as surely as she knew her own name.

For weeks, her mind had battled her gut instinct. Logic dictated that she move her coven to safety. Still, her instinct had urged her to stay. She hadn't had any more visions of Blackbeard, but that fact gave her no hope at all. She was a new queen, untrained in the ways of the amulet, and utterly incapable of having a proper, reliable vision, as far as she was concerned.

Despite news of Blackbeard's pardon by Governor Eden, stories still circulated about his illicit endeavors along the coast. Charlotte sought out as much information as she could each time she visited the waterfront. Fishermen often gave the best details, but sometimes a vendor would offer up a plausible story to help fill in the gaps of her knowledge regarding the pirate's activities.

Her mind swirled with the latest collection of tales. One fisherman had mentioned that Blackbeard now camped in Ocracoke with his crew. Another had told her that he'd settled in Bath with a new wife and a baby on the way. But the fabric vendor swore she knew that the pirate was still very active and had now taken to more land-based robberies. She'd insisted that her own cousin's farm had been raided by his men.

Charlotte couldn't know which of the stories were true. Perhaps they all were.

A salty breeze drifted in from the water, and she took a moment to breathe it in as best she could against the pinch of her whalebone stays. She had not yet grown accustomed to the petticoats and cumbersome skirts that she wore to blend in with the other women of the town. Though they still felt very much like a fancy costume to her, she had tried her best not to show her discomfort.

"Hello!" William called to her as she approached the construction lot.

Standing next to a stack of pine shingles, he beamed. "What do you think?" He gestured at the unfinished house with his arms open wide.

With its outer shell nearly complete, it was clear this would be a grand home. She could easily envision its splendor when it was finally completed. Though she came from a long line of queens, she doubted any of her ancestors had enjoyed such luxury.

"It's shaping up nicely."

"We'll have it all closed in soon." William puffed out his chest. "After we get the windows and shutters placed, I might ask you to venture in to add some feminine touches."

Charlotte bit her lip. She knew nothing about decorating… and apparently that was something she was supposed to know.

As much as she'd tried to fit in, she still felt out of place among the women of the town. The world outside her home village was far more peculiar than she'd expected it would be. She'd been raised to be a leader, but here—as far as anyone else knew—she must spend her time wearing pretty dresses and providing tasteful decoration for someone else's home.

"I look forward to that." She gave him a sideways glance. "It really is quite lovely."

The captain pulled off his hat and wiped the sweat from his brow. "I'm glad you like it."

Charlotte opened her basket and began to lay out the captain's lunch atop the stout cart he used to transport materials to the site.

"Thank you." He eyed the cornbread, salted fish, wild strawberries, and cheese with appreciation before sitting down beside her. "This looks delicious."

She popped a strawberry in her mouth as they both took seats on nearby crates.

"I heard that Blackbeard has gone and found himself a wife." She couldn't very well tell him that she'd had a prophetic vision of the pirate approaching her on the *Annabelle*, so she kept her voice as lighthearted and conversational as she could manage. "Isn't that curious?"

"From what I've heard, that beast of a man found himself *numerous* wives. I believe the current one is his fourteenth." He bit off a hunk of cornbread.

Charlotte wondered if she, Hannah, and Cate had been included in that count. The thought chased away any appetite she'd had for lunch.

"No. What I mean is, they say he's given up pirating altogether. Found a wife and settled down. He may even be expecting a wee one."

"A scoundrel like him? He may have taken another wife, but he definitely hasn't settled down," William scoffed. "I know that much for a fact."

Charlotte raised an eyebrow. "What are you saying?"

"You really shouldn't concern yourself with such things."

She jumped to her feet in an instant.

William watched her with wide eyes. "What's the matter?"

"I will concern myself with whatever I damn well please." Glaring, she crossed her arms. "And I'll thank you not to suggest otherwise."

She'd had quite enough of corsets, and needlepoint, and not concerning herself with "such things." Charlotte pressed her lips in a tight line and watched the color drain from William's cheeks.

"Oh…well…I." He ran his hand through his hair. "I didn't mean—"

"What do you know of his whereabouts?"

The captain dusted the cornbread crumbs from his hands and stood up. "He is anchored at Ocracoke. We have confirmed it."

"All these months, I've listened to rumors about where he's been and what he might do next. I search for him along the waterfront—"

William studied her with a puzzled expression. "Charlotte, what on earth were you planning to do if you had known where he was?"

"I don't know!" She regretted those words as soon as they burst from her mouth. But they were true. That much she couldn't deny.

"Don't you see?" He reached for her hands, but she jerked away from him. "I didn't want to subject you to needless worry."

She narrowed her eyes. "I am perfectly capable of deciding what I should and shouldn't worry about."

"I see your point." He dipped his head, offering her a subtle bow. "Forgive me."

Charlotte thought his remorse seemed genuine, but she couldn't quite let go of her anger just yet. "I'll forgive you… provided you never withhold information about Blackbeard again."

With a nod, the captain stepped back to his crate and took a seat. "What else would you like to know?"

"Everything." She sat down beside him. "Have you alerted the Royal Navy of his location?"

"It's more complicated than that." He picked up his cornbread.

"I'll do my best to keep up." She made no effort to mask her irritation.

He raised his hands, cornbread and all. "I wasn't suggesting—"

"It's all right." Seeing his embarrassment, she dismissed the issue with flick of her wrist. "Please, continue with what you were about to say."

"Well…" He heaved a wary sigh. "We would need the governor to order the Navy to confront him, and that won't happen because Eden is in cahoots with him. We believe that's why Blackbeard received his pardon."

"Oh." Charlotte curled inward, shoulders slumped in defeat. "Isn't there someone who can help?"

"There is." The captain exhaled, long and deep, as if he knew he'd regret what he was about to say. "Me."

Her mouth ran dry. "Are you suggesting that you will confront him?"

"I have already begun purchasing arms and recruiting men for the mission. It will take some time to get organized…but yes, we are preparing to end piracy in this region ourselves."

She jumped back onto her feet and began to pace.

William stood up as well. "Did I say something wrong again?"

Charlotte couldn't look at him. "I can't bear the thought of a fight with him and his crew. Someone could get hurt. *You* could get hurt."

"I hate to see you like this. What can I do to ease your worries?"

Charlotte bit her tongue. She couldn't "not worry." Blackbeard had stolen so much already. She wouldn't let him take William too.

Chapter twenty-one

L ate that night, Charlotte extinguished the lone candle on her bedside table and rested her head against her pillow. She could tell by their uneven breathing that neither of her companions had dozed off yet. By now, Cate would have listened to her memories of her conversation with William. It had swirled through her mind countless times since she'd returned to the Sutherland estate.

She had made no effort to shield her thoughts from Cate. The young witch needed to know everything so she could listen for any pertinent information that may go unspoken among Beaufort's residents. In particular, Charlotte worried that William would leave her in the dark in an effort to protect her delicate feminine sensibilities.

She pulled the coverlet up to her chin and sighed. *William.* He had been so good to her, and to Hannah and Cate as well. But when it came to treating her as an equal, he had quite a lot to learn.

"You'll feel better if you talk to us about it," Cate murmured in the darkness.

"Yes. You should tell us what's wrong." Hannah rolled onto her side with a groan. "I may not have Cate's gift, but your worries are keeping me up too."

After a moment's hesitation, Charlotte shared all that she'd learned about the prickly politics surrounding Blackbeard and his current too close for comfort location.

"Then we should just leave." Hannah spoke with a jarring certainty. "The weather will change any day now. We already knew he would come here, and now we know he's protected by the governor. We're asking for trouble if we stay."

Charlotte touched the invisible amulet on her chest. "I think there might be a way—"

"You care more about William than you do for our safety!"

Wincing from the pain of Hannah's accusation, Charlotte bolted upright in her bed. "That's not true. Yes, I'm worried for him. But you two are my greatest priority. You always will be."

"Please Hannah, try to stay calm," Cate said in the gentlest of tones. "I can assure you, she has not shirked her duty as our queen."

Charlotte held her tongue. As much as she appreciated Cate's defense, her own word alone should have been enough to convince Hannah. But then again, she understood her friend's doubts. She hadn't earned her trust yet. And Charlotte knew she never would unless she found a way to end the threat of Blackbeard for good.

In the quiet of the darkened room, she considered all the ways she'd prefer to end the threat. She imagined striking his boat with a fire ball and watching the wooden vessel explode into a thousand burning pieces. She toyed with idea of fighting him herself and using all of her powerful magic to bring him to his knees. She'd watch him beg for his life, for his own safety, and she would laugh in his grizzled face.

But every idea she had involved the risk of revealing herself as a witch. If she were discovered, Hannah and Cate would immediately be presumed guilty by association. And then they'd be in just as much danger facing a throng of angry townspeople as they'd be if Blackbeard found them again.

After a while, Hannah began her soft snoring, as she did every night before her nightmares began. Charlotte closed her eyes with the hope of finding sleep herself. But her mind continued to wander over impossible options and outright fantasies.

But one idea came to her. One that might just work. Excited by the thought, she opened her eyes.

Cate pulled her coverlet back. "I can help you with that."

"I need to think on it some more…work out all the details," Charlotte said. "Rest now. We'll take care of it tomorrow."

Chapter twenty-two

November 1718

Charlotte worked on her needlepoint beside the sitting room's crackling fire. Mother Sutherland and Cate did the same, as the quiet activity had become part of their evening routine.

Hannah, citing a fervent desire to rest after a long day of relaxing, had already retired to her room. Charlotte knew her friend wasn't the least bit sleepy. She'd simply found a perfect excuse to avoid practicing her embroidery.

As much as Charlotte would have preferred to do so, she couldn't dwell on Hannah's clever avoidance tactic. Instead, her thoughts drifted to William. He'd gone to meet with his father in the study earlier that evening and had yet to come back to her. Though she hoped the men were busy discussing the *Annabelle*'s sailing schedule, she couldn't help but worry that their talks involved something far less mundane.

She cast a sideways glance at Cate, who drove her needle with precision. No hint of alarm darkened the young witch's expression as she practiced her embroidery with a steady hand. But then again, the captain and his father were too far away for her to read their thoughts.

An angry shout boomed from deep inside the house.

Charlotte couldn't make out the words, but she recognized the voice right away. *William.*

Mother Sutherland froze with her needle poised to puncture her linen cloth. After a moment, when no additional disturbances came, she continued with her work as if nothing had happened. Charlotte turned to Cate, who only offered a subtle shrug to indicate that she still could not hear the men's thoughts.

Charlotte bit her lip and tried to concentrate on her embroidery, but it swam, unfocused, in her hands. She wanted to run to the study and find out what had made William so angry he'd yelled. She'd never heard him raise his voice before. It had to be something serious to illicit such a response from him.

While she had explained to William that he shouldn't shield her from matters typically handled by the menfolk, Charlotte suspected the other members of the Sutherland household wouldn't share her view that women were just as capable as men. The last thing she needed right now was to cause a stir, so she had no choice but to continue feigning fascination with her needlepoint.

At long last, she heard the hard thump of the captain's boots as he exited the study and stomped down the hall. He softened his steps as he neared the sitting room, and by the time he finally came into view, he appeared completely calm.

But there was a darkness in his eyes. Charlotte could see it from all the way across the room. She whipped her gaze back to Cate, who gripped her embroidery needle in a trembling hand. The color had drained from her cheeks.

"Having a lovely evening, I hope." The captain forced a smile as he looked at Charlotte from the doorway. "I have to step out for a bit, but I'll be back soon." He turned on his heel and marched toward the front door.

Charlotte dropped her embroidery on the floor and hurried after him. By the time she reached the foyer, he had already closed the door on his way out. She swung it open.

"William, wait!"

He stopped on the last porch step. "You should go in. It's chilly tonight. You'll catch a cold."

She didn't care at all about the cold as she rushed to his side. "Please...you have to tell me what's going on. I know you're angry about something."

"I apologize if I ruined your restful evening." He placed a consoling hand on her shoulder. "But this is nothing for you to worry yourself—"

Charlotte silenced him with a look.

She hated being left in the dark as much as she hated being relegated to the womanly world of needlepoint. Such an arrangement might be satisfactory for the mainland women, but where she came from, that wasn't the case. Charlotte was a queen, and she had a job to do.

"It's Blackbeard, isn't it?" She refused to back down.

William furrowed his brow. "I really must go see Turner."

She had heard him speak of Turner before and knew he was a town leader. The captain wouldn't go to him at this late hour if it weren't a matter of utmost importance.

"I do not require protection from bad news, William. You should know that by now." She raised her chin in defiance. "I insist that you tell me what's going on."

"You're not like any of the other women here." The captain remained silent for a long moment, looking at her as if he were seeing her for the first time. "But this *is* truly distressing news..."

Charlotte threw her arms up in frustration and glared at him.

William gave a defeated sigh. "Blackbeard's holding some sort of celebration in Ocracoke with other pirates and their crews. It's been going on for some time now. We've spied on them while we've readied our own weaponry and men. But we've just received word that he's been gathering supplies to set sail again." He eyed her with caution before continuing. "We'll have to act fast if we are to catch him."

"I see." Even as the shiver raced up her spine, Charlotte maintained a calm façade. William had trusted her with the information, and she didn't want to risk any semblance of weakness in light of the news. "What happened with your father? Why were you angry?"

"He tried to persuade me not to lead this mission. He believes our men will be massacred by those pirates." The captain raised his chin. "But I, as you must have heard, wholeheartedly disagree."

Charlotte studied his tight shoulders and rigid jawline. "When will you go?"

"As soon as possible." He stood tall and squared shouldered. "My *Annabelle* is nearly ready with suitable weaponry, and my men will gladly fight by my side. All that's left to handle are minor details."

The only thing worse than knowing that the threat of Blackbeard continued was the knowledge that the captain would so willingly put himself in harm's way. She couldn't bear the thought. "William…"

"When I think of all that he took from you and your sisters…" His eyes flashed with determination. "If I have to start a war to end that demon, I will."

Knowing she couldn't change his mind, Charlotte stepped closer to him and rested her head against his chest. He wrapped his arms around her.

After a moment, he pulled away. "You're shivering in this night air. Please go inside and warm yourself by the fire."

Charlotte made her way back up the porch steps and then peered over her shoulder to watch William march down the street, determined. With a knot in her stomach, she swung open the door and almost bumped into Cate, who'd been waiting for her in the foyer.

When Cate's mouth fell open, Charlotte knew her thoughts revealed all the trouble that was to come.

"But I think your letter will work. We just need more time." The young witch buried her face in her hands.

The letter. Charlotte had hinged all their plans for the future on it and had allowed her friends to stay in Beaufort on borrowed time while she awaited its results.

She recalled the night she'd sent it as clearly as if it had just happened, but in reality, nearly a month had passed since then. After learning that the governor was in cahoots with Blackbeard, she'd drafted a letter—identifying herself only as an anonymous resident of Beaufort. In it, she had divulged the pirate's location and detailed his many crimes, as if there were any chance that the recipient hadn't heard of him.

Whoever that recipient might be.

Charlotte didn't know who might receive it or when they would. She didn't know who could act on the information she had shared. She only knew that their governor wouldn't. On that dark night when she'd opened her window and held the folded parchment into the breeze, she'd used her magic to send the letter to someone—anyone—who could defeat Blackbeard and his men.

"What has happened?" Hannah appeared at the top of the staircase.

Charlotte closed her eyes and sighed before climbing the staircase, where she could answer the question without being overheard. "Blackbeard is preparing to set sail again, and the captain intends to stop him."

Hannah watched her with a narrowed gaze. "I don't think the captain can defeat Blackbeard."

"I don't either," Charlotte confessed.

Cate climbed the last of the steps and stood beside them. "But someone needs to defeat him."

Charlotte nodded and touched the invisible amulet on her chest. "I need some time to think. Perhaps after a good rest, I'll be able to see a solution."

But she had no doubt there would be very little sleep for her that night.

Chapter twenty-three

When the sun began to rise and illuminate their room, Charlotte glanced over at Hannah, who was also wide awake and staring at the ceiling. She had cupped a protective hand over her swelling belly as sweat beaded on her forehead. Her haunted expression told Charlotte everything she needed to know.

She'd had another nightmare.

Mumbling something incoherent in her sleep, Cate rolled onto her side. Charlotte wondered if nervousness about Blackbeard had invaded her slumber as well.

She lay in bed for a few minutes more before rising and getting dressed. By the time she'd made herself presentable, both Hannah and Cate were out of their beds as well.

Charlotte peered through the window to see that the red strokes of sunrise had begun to give way to blue sky. "I want to go check on William. He's probably gone to the docks by now."

Hannah patted her stomach. "The bigger I get, the less the Sutherland women let me do. I think I'll get an earful if I try to leave."

"It's still early yet." Charlotte wrapped a shawl around her shoulders. "If we hurry, we can walk right out while they sleep."

Cate tied on her bonnet. "Yes. Let's go."

Managing to stay quieter than the clatter provided by the kitchen servants, the three of them shuffled right out of the house and began the short walk to the waterfront. Not a single cloud floated in the sky overhead, but the unfettered sunshine wasn't quite enough to chase away the fall chill in the air. Charlotte quickened her pace in an effort to stay warm.

Cate grimaced. "Jasper is among the captain's men."

"I know." Charlotte stroked her arm. "I'm sorry."

"I cannot imagine a more dangerous endeavor for him." Cate shook her head. "He's brave and strong, but Blackbeard and his men are so…"

She didn't finish her sentence. She didn't have to. Charlotte knew the feeling all too well.

"There must be something *we* can do to stop Blackbeard." Hannah's cheeks flushed red with anger. "To have this power and not be able to use it is maddening."

"I want him stopped too," Charlotte said. "But we cannot risk exposure, and I just don't see how it can be done safely. Everything we do must be hidden in explainable causes. The sandbar we created appeared to be a natural phenomenon. Even that letter I sent was designed to blend in with other messages the recipient might receive."

"The magic we used to quell your morning sickness was simple and only affected you, so we were safe to use it," Cate added.

Hannah stroked her belly. "I…I didn't know you did that."

Charlotte nodded as she remembered the simple spell they'd used to help Hannah—just a mixture of tea and magical intent to help their suffering friend.

"I learned that one from my mother," Cate said to Hannah. "We put a strand of your hair in the peppermint tea and focused on your wellness."

"I am grateful for your help." Hannah smiled at them. "I wouldn't have accepted it had you offered."

"We know." Charlotte and Cate answered in unison.

On any other day, the moment might have brought about a giggle from each of them. But on this morning, laughter was the furthest thing from Charlotte's mind. And she suspected that Hannah and Cate felt the same way.

They noticed more residents moving about as they neared the waterfront. The baker had already opened his shop, and from the scent of warm, baking bread wafting their way, he'd been at work for a long while. A few fishermen boarded a small vessel and began to row away from the dock while an early bird vendor set up his display in the open-air market.

But all of that activity slipped into the background when Charlotte laid her eyes on the *Annabelle*. Right away, she spotted the bustling activity all around the ship. More men than she'd seen during her entire stay on board moved about the deck now, some with pistols and others with daggers. Five young crewmen struggled to pull a cannon up the gangplank.

Just like that, the *Annabelle* was no longer a merchant vessel. She'd become a warship.

Charlotte could hardly hear the shouts of the men over the pounding of her own heartbeat.

"Good morning, ladies!" The captain waved at them from the dock before jogging over to them. "Have you come to watch all the commotion?"

She couldn't bring herself to mimic his jovial mood. All of a sudden, the nagging anxiety which had haunted her since he first mentioned his intentions evolved into something more— something she couldn't will away from her mind. She saw him slumped on a ship's deck. Blood oozed from his chest, creating a creeping crimson stain across his crisp, white shirt.

Blackbeard stood over William's dying body, grinning.

She gasped at the thought. That wasn't mere anxiety. That was a vision, just like the one she'd had of Blackbeard coming for her on the deck of the *Annabelle*. Unable to speak, she stared at him.

William cocked his head. "Charlotte, my dear, are you quite all right?"

"Oh…yes…I…just…" She wanted to grab him and beg him not to go. It was all she could do to keep from telling him exactly why he shouldn't go after Blackbeard.

Cate came to her rescue. "When do you plan to leave?"

"Tomorrow, God willing." He pointed to the work going on aboard the *Annabelle*. "My men are ready. And, we've heard that Blackbeard is hosting a massive party—it's been going on for days. He's invited even more of his fiendish peers to join him as well. So, there's a good chance we'll be able to put a few more pirates out of business…especially if we are able to surprise them."

But Charlotte knew there was no chance of that. No chance at all. It would be a massacre, and the captain—with all his courage, honor, and limitless pride—would be one of the first to fall. She stared hard at him, unable to reconcile his excitement with the tragedy she knew was imminent. "I don't think you should go. There must be another way."

"Captain!" A crewman called to him from the *Annabelle*'s deck. "We need you up here."

"I have to go." William reached out and grabbed her hands, giving them a squeeze. "Don't fret. Soon we'll have this monster out of our hair for good."

She watched him race back to his ship, wishing the whole time that she could just use her magic to bind him on land.

Cate stroked Charlotte's arm. "Are you all right?"

"I...I don't think I'll ever see him again." Charlotte tried to hold herself together, but she couldn't keep her lip from quivering. "I wish I knew what to do."

"I have an idea," Hannah said.

Chapter twenty-four

Charlotte made her way to the waterfront the next morning. With each step forward, her fear for William's safety deepened. She could only hope this wouldn't be the last time she'd see him alive. Cate matched her brisk pace but stayed silent as the *Annabelle* came into view.

"You can go back to the house to help Hannah gather the supplies." She gestured in the direction of the Sutherland estate. "I can handle this on my own."

Cate stayed by her side. "We're all in this together, aren't we?"

Mother chose my companions well. She gave Cate a grateful half-smile and pressed on.

"Did you see Jasper yesterday?" Charlotte asked after a quiet moment.

With a sad wince, Cate nodded.

"We still have Hannah's plan to try." She touched her young friend's arm in an effort to provide comfort that she didn't feel herself.

The new plan wasn't foolproof. They all knew it. But with no results from Charlotte's letter, it gave the captain and his men their best chance of survival in what would surely be a bloody battle.

When they neared the waterfront, they noticed the whirl of activity on the docks. Most of the men of the town had volunteered for the dangerous mission. And now, as those men boarded the newly armed *Annabelle*, they said their goodbyes to their tearful wives and children who had gathered to see them off. Tension hung in the air, thick and oppressive, as grim-faced crewmen prepared the vessel for its departure.

After spotting William directing the flurry of activity on the dock, Charlotte attempted to steel herself while he finished giving some instruction to a young volunteer. He wore the same crisp, white shirt she'd seen in her vision. She managed to hold back her tears, but she couldn't bring herself to pretend to be happy as they walked toward each other.

As always, the captain had an air of cool confidence. Under normal circumstances, Charlotte found that demeanor alluring. But today—of all days—it scared her. His pride would soon drive his bravery into recklessness, and he would pay the ultimate price for it.

"I still think you should stay here." It was all she could manage to say without sobbing.

"You know I can't do that." He gazed into her eyes for a long moment and then cupped her cheeks in his hands. "You'll see me tomorrow."

She didn't speak. She couldn't.

He bent down and planted a kiss on her forehead.

Jasper suddenly burst through the crowded dock and ran over to William.

"Sir...the contingent has arrived. They wait for us just beyond the harbor!" Jasper gasped for air, his chest heaving from the effort.

"Excellent news." The captain shifted his attention back to Charlotte. "Lieutenant Maynard has come from Virginia with two ships to assist us."

Charlotte stared at him with wide eyes. "I didn't know you'd have help."

"I didn't either. Not till just yesterday when the messenger came to inform me." He shrugged, seeming baffled by the series of events. "It seems he received a letter notifying him of Blackbeard's location. Unlike our Governor Eden, he's eager to put the pirate out of business and has requested our assistance."

So, her message had found its intended recipient. But not soon enough to keep William safely on land in Beaufort.

"There's no need for all of you to go if he's sending two vessels of his own." Charlotte knew those words were a waste of breath before she uttered them.

"Oh, but we must. The Ocracoke party's been going on for a long time, with more and more joining in each day." William straightened his cap. "There's no telling how many pirates are out there now. I can't just stand by while Maynard sails his men into that."

Jasper beamed at him. "Captain Sutherland has it all sorted out. We're going to board Maynard's ships. And we'll leave some of the crew on the *Annabelle* for extra support if we need it."

"The *Ranger* and the *Jane* are smaller vessels. They can navigate the shallow waters better than my *Annabelle*." William's eyes sparkled as he laid out his plan. "We'll all be hidden below deck, so Blackbeard won't know how many of us there are until it's too late."

She glanced at his chest, at the fabric of his pristine shirt, and blinked in an attempt to push away the vision that refused to leave her. But the bloody stain wouldn't budge.

William reached for Charlotte's hand. "Try not to worry."

Cate let out a high-pitched cry and launched herself into Jasper's arms. "Be careful!" She buried her head in his neck until the captain tugged on the young man's shoulders, reminding him that there was work to do.

"Time to go." William kept his voice stern when he spoke to Jasper, but there was a gentleness about him when he turned to Charlotte. "I'll see you tomorrow." He gave her another sweet kiss, this time on her cheek.

As Charlotte and Cate watched the two men walk back to the *Annabelle*, the younger witch sniffed and wiped away a tear. "Do you think they'll come home to us?"

"We'll do everything we can to make that happen."

Chapter twenty-five

Though Charlotte, Cate, and Hannah were all anxious to enact their plan, they had to wait until the Sutherland household quieted down after dinner. Charlotte feigned exhaustion from fretting over William and excused herself from the evening's needlepoint work in order to meet Hannah upstairs in their room.

Rising from her seat, Charlotte glanced at Cate. *Wait a few minutes, then take your leave as well. Tell Mother Sutherland you want to check on me.*

Cate continued her stitches but gave a slight nod to acknowledge the instructions.

It took everything Charlotte had to pretend to trudge up the staircase when all she wanted to do was run to her room and get started on the spell. But she kept the charade going until she made it to the door. When she pushed it open, she found Hannah waiting for her.

"Did you get everything?" she whispered after she closed the door behind her.

Hannah nodded. "Where's Cate?"

"She'll be along soon." Charlotte watched Hannah kneel down with an awkward grunt. "Here let me help you."

"I think you're starting to adopt the mainlanders' sensitivities." Hannah shooed her away before pulling a beeswax candle and a glass bottle filled with rum from beneath the bed. "I'm only pregnant. I'm not an invalid."

Charlotte eyed the brown liquid in the jar and remembered the scent of the liquor on Blackbeard's foul breath. She grimaced at the memory. "I wish we could make this spell stronger somehow. From this distance and without—"

"I have something else to show you." Hannah propped her hand on the bedside and pulled herself to her feet. "I kept it from you because I feared you would throw it away. After all, there's only one good use for it."

With an arched brow, she watched her friend stride back to the dresser and open a drawer.

Hannah reached all the way to the back of it and rummaged around. "I almost threw it away myself at one point because I thought I wouldn't be able to use my magic in this new life of ours. But now I'm glad I kept it." She rotated back around slowly. "And I think you will be too."

Charlotte's jaw dropped when Hannah opened her hand, revealing the item she'd held in secret since their abduction—a black ribbon with strands of greasy black hair caught up in the knot.

"Is that *his?*"

"Mm-hmm." Hannah smirked with pride. "I took it from his quarters."

Charlotte opened her mouth to speak, but nothing came out.

Cate burst into the room and closed the door behind her. Her full skirt fanned out around her as she spun to face them. Catching sight of the ribbon in Hannah's hand, she clamped her hand over her mouth. Her eyes lit up. "Oh! You still have it? I'd forgotten about that."

"You knew?" Charlotte shook her head. "Of course you knew."

Cate twisted the lock on the doorknob while Hannah drew the curtains closed. With her heart pounding, Charlotte double-checked the lock. *Can't be too careful.*

Charlotte ran through the plan in her mind to make sure they wouldn't miss anything. They had to get it right. First, they'd capitalize on the Ocracoke party by using their magic to propel the pirates into drunkenness. Some, she knew, would overindulge just fine on their own. But others—maybe even Blackbeard himself—might stay alert enough to fight with lethal effect.

And that simply wouldn't do.

Now, with Hannah's addition of Blackbeard's hair, they could target their magic even better. But Charlotte knew, even with that added assurance, the sheer number of pirates in the mix now could render their spell almost useless.

But if we can weaken their leader...

She could make no guarantee that William would walk away from this fight unscathed, but she clung to her deep and steadfast hope that he would.

Cate grabbed the bottle of rum and placed it on their little table while Hannah used her magic to light the candle. Raising her hand to her amulet, Charlotte released it from its disguising spell. It glowed against her skin, warm and powerful. For just a moment, she felt as though her mother was right there with them. Would she be proud of the path they'd chosen?

Charlotte thought she might.

All three stepped forward, forming a circle around the table. Hannah uncorked the rum and held Blackbeard's ribbon above it, hesitating for just a quick beat before dropping the vile thing into the bottle.

After Hannah replaced the cork, Charlotte sealed it in place with wax from the burning candle and then set it back down on the table. Everything was ready.

They joined hands, just as they had in the hold of the *Queen Anne's Revenge*. Charlotte felt the light of her magic envelop her as the amethyst glowed even brighter to bolster their combined powers.

She led the familiar chant. "One mind, one spirit, one focus."

Charlotte envisioned the intent of the spell. A drunken Blackbeard, groggy and slurring his words, surrounded by crewmen in the same condition. Clumsy and unprepared, they'd struggle to wield their swords and muskets.

Magic swirled through their circle and surrounded the bottle before disappearing in a flash.

Charlotte took a deep breath. "It is done."

"It is done," Cate and Hannah echoed.

"And now we must wait." Charlotte strode to the window and pulled the curtains apart. Looking out at the moon, she wondered if she'd been able to spare William's life with the spell.

Morning couldn't come soon enough.

chapter twenty-six

A s she waited for daybreak, Charlotte lay in her bed with a tight grip on the amulet. She'd dozed in fits throughout the night, in a state of constant wonder and worry, and she knew Cate had done the same. She'd heard the young witch toss and turn all through the dark hours. Among them, only Hannah had enjoyed any real rest. And now, as sky began to lighten in the presence of the rising sun, her soft snores provided the only sound in the room.

Charlotte waited a few more excruciating minutes before pushing off her covers and rising to her feet. The wooden floorboards were cold against her bare toes, but she hastened to wash her face and get dressed.

Seeming just as eager to seek out information about the captain's mission and to learn of Jasper's fate, Cate sprung from her bed as well. They were both in the process of tying on their bonnets when Hannah finally stirred.

She blinked at them. "Where are you off to so early?"

"To the harbor. I want to be there the minute the *Annabelle* returns." Frowning, Charlotte smoothed the bodice of her dress. She'd had no more visions of William—nothing to indicate whether or not their magic had saved him.

"That is, *if* it returns." Cate furrowed her brow.

Hannah threw off her coverlet. "I'll join you." Skipping a corset altogether, she readied herself faster than they had. "Let's go."

With the exception of the early morning bustle of kitchen servants, the house remained quiet. But Charlotte suspected Mother Sutherland and William's sisters would join them at the dock as soon as they woke.

With quick strides, the three witches made their way to the waterfront and found that they weren't the only early risers that day. Dozens of wives and mothers stood waiting for their loved ones to come home. Some had even hauled their rocking chairs to the dock, as if they expected a long, uneasy day ahead.

It might have looked like a party had it not been for the somber mood. Charlotte took in the sight of the yawning, empty expanse at the dock—where the *Annabelle* had floated just the day before. The strange and unsettling sight only added to her anxiety. She touched a hand to her nervous stomach, hoping with all her heart that good news would come soon.

Cate shifted her weight from one foot to another while Hannah stood stock still, her arms crossed over her rounded belly. The sun rose higher, illuminating them with its full morning glow, as even more of the town's residents came to wait for the *Annabelle*'s arrival.

Finally, a little boy's voice rose up from the crowd. "There it is! I see it!" He pointed his finger to a far-off dot sailing on the water.

Charlotte bit her lip as an excited murmur rose up from the crowd. Without being able to see the souls on board, no one celebrated yet. They could only wait as it drew closer, hoping their loved ones had survived the excursion.

She spotted its intact sails first and took a cautious comfort in the notion that the ship had not sustained any obvious damage. But that knowledge provided no guarantee that William was safe. From this distance, she couldn't even tell if the men of Beaufort were on board the vessel. For all she knew, Blackbeard and his crew had stolen the *Annabelle* and were now en route to exact their revenge on the town.

She closed her eyes and concentrated on her breathing. Any moment now, she would know William's fate.

"I think it's them," Hannah said.

Charlotte opened her eyes to view the approaching ship. She couldn't yet make out the faces of the men on the *Annabelle*'s deck, but several of them had lined up along the railing and raised their arms in a fervent greeting to all the people waiting on the waterfront—a most unpirate-like behavior.

"I see my Jasper!" Cate bounced up on her toes.

Hannah and Charlotte exchanged a hopeful glance as Cate buzzed with excited glee.

The crowd on the dock erupted in cheers and applause, but Charlotte couldn't look away from the ship. Was William on board? The vision she'd had of his bloody demise lurked in her mind. She clasped her hands together and continued to scan the faces of the crewmen. She didn't see him anywhere.

"But he sees you." Cate flashed a knowing grin.

Hannah pointed at the bow of the ship. "There he is."

Charlotte followed their gazes. Some of the crewmen at the railing suddenly shifted to make room for their captain. William stood tall and proud in their midst, but he stared at her as if she were the only person on the waterfront. He brought his hand to his lips and blew her a kiss.

Her knees wobbled, nearly giving out beneath her, but she managed to greet him with a bright smile.

"You two are silly." Cate giggled. "So prim and proper."

"It is his way." Charlotte watched the *Annabelle* coast into her position at the dock, hoping to catch another glimpse of William. "And I don't mind it at all."

"I don't think I could stand it." Cate sighed as she tucked a wayward lock of hair into her bonnet and then squared her shoulders. "In fact, I think I shall I ask my Jasper to marry me the minute he steps off that boat."

Charlotte whipped her head around. "You'll do no such thing. You barely know him. Besides, you're far too young for that!"

The teenager raised her chin. "You are not my mother."

Hannah scoffed as if she knew how this conversation would end.

Charlotte narrowed her eyes. "No, but I am your *queen*."

Hannah gave Charlotte a playful nudge while Cate pouted.

The first of the crewmen and volunteers began to make their way down the gangplank and into the arms of their waiting wives and children. Enthusiastic voices rose up as the townspeople's questions were met with prideful tales of chivalry. While Charlotte waited for William to disembark, she listened for news of Blackbeard's fate.

Jasper appeared on the gangplank and searched the crowd for Cate, who spotted him right away.

"Over here!" She raised her hand and wiggled her fingers.

He darted their way, his cheeks flushed with excitement. Cate let out a joyful squeal and wrapped her arms around him as soon as he was within reach.

Hannah took a hesitant step forward as he peeled himself out of Cate's enthusiastic embrace. "Blackbeard...is he dead?"

"Indeed, he is!" Jasper gave them a jubilant nod. "It took twenty wounds from a cutlass and five pistol shots to put an end to that devil. Saw what became of him with my own eyes." He jabbed his thumb toward his puffed out chest. "They cut his head off to make sure he was dead, and then they threw his body overboard."

Though the image brought a certain revulsion to Charlotte, she couldn't deny she was glad to hear it. When she looked at Hannah, she noticed a slow, steady smile spread across her friend's face.

It is done.

"One of Maynard's men saw Blackbeard's body swim around the ship three times searching for his head." Punctuating it with a confident nod, Jasper relayed this information as if it were an incontrovertible fact.

"That seems unlikely." Hannah's lips curled with unabashed amusement.

Jasper shrugged. "If anyone could have done such a thing, it would have been Blackbeard."

Charlotte searched the crowd for William and spotted him stepping off the gangplank, his eyes already fixed on her. As she raced forward to meet him, she saw that he held his hand clamped down at his side and moved with an undeniable stiffness.

She came to an abrupt stop when she reached him. "You are injured!"

"It's only a flesh wound." He stroked her cheek with his free hand, paying no mind to the blood stain on his shirt. "And an embarrassing one at that."

Puzzled, Charlotte cocked her head and waited for him to continue.

"It was Blackbeard who nicked me. But the scoundrel was so drunk, he could barely swing his cutlass." He wore a sheepish grin as he met her curious gaze. "The fact that he managed to hit me at all is a failure on my part."

She stifled a laugh. "Well then, we'll just leave that part out of the story."

"Yes, I think we'll do just that." He pressed his lips against hers. "I'm so glad to come home to you."

Chapter twenty-seven

March 1719

"Push!" Charlotte gripped Hannah's hand as she coached her friend through the final stages of hard labor.

The pains had started that morning. And now, just past dinnertime, the entire household awaited the baby's arrival. Charlotte knew the Sutherland women, who milled about at the bottom of the stairs, looked forward to greeting Beaufort's newest resident. But to her, this child would begin the next generation of the people she was sworn to protect.

Hannah's raven hair clung to her perspiring face as she gritted her teeth and bore down as hard as she could.

"That's it...you can do it!" Cate popped up from beneath the sheet they'd draped across Hannah's knees. "Almost done!" She beamed at Charlotte and then ducked back down to finish her work.

Then came the wail—a healthy, powerful cry.

Awestruck, Charlotte watched Hannah sink with exhaustion against her pillow. "Well done!"

"Such a handsome boy!" Cate proclaimed as she wrapped the fussy bundle in a blanket and presented him to his mother.

The baby already had a tuft of thick, black hair atop his head. From Hannah, Charlotte decided right away, not Blackbeard. "I think he looks like you."

The new mother gave a tired laugh as she lovingly stroked the little one's soft cheek. "I will call him Henry."

"That's a fine name for a fine boy." Cate zipped to Hannah's side with a cool, damp cloth and dabbed the sweat from her forehead.

Hannah's expression darkened as she looked down at her son. "He doesn't have a father."

"No, he doesn't." Charlotte rose to her feet. "He has us though, and we'll help you both every step of the way."

Hugging her baby close, she gave a hesitant smile. "So, you would accept him—even if he's not like us?"

Charlotte had wondered all along if the child would inherit Hannah's gifts or if he would be just like any of the other mainlanders. Now, as she took in the sight of this new life, she realized that didn't matter at all. Of course she hoped he would share their magic. But even if he didn't, she'd love him just the same. She placed her hand across Henry's plump belly and blessed his arrival without reservation.

Chapter twenty-eight

With mother and baby resting in comfort under the watchful gaze of Cate and all the other doting women of the Sutherland house, Charlotte stole away for a quiet walk along the waterfront. The chill of winter had surrendered to the promise of a warm spring, so she let her shawl hang open as she inhaled the salty air blowing in from the harbor.

She stopped when she came to William's grand new house. Painted white with black shutters, it stood two stories tall and had wide front porches on both floors. She could almost see herself sitting in a rocking chair on one of those porches, taking in the view of a brilliant sunset while chatting the evening away with the captain—just as she'd done so many times during her stay aboard the *Annabelle*.

He'd completed the construction several weeks earlier but had yet to move in. He hadn't asked her to marry him yet either.

She frowned. *I wonder if he ever will.*

"Where do you go with those faraway thoughts?"

Charlotte, jolted back into the moment, looked up to see William descend the porch steps and head her way. "Oh, I didn't know you were here today."

He dusted off his hands as he came to a stop in front of her. "Just putting up a few finishing touches on the new house."

She stifled a grin, unable to imagine the captain fussing about paint or curtains. "Finishing touches?"

He glanced back at the home with a wrinkle in his brow. "I wanted it to be perfect, and I think, at long last, I've accomplished that."

"I'm sure it's just fine. It looks beautiful from here."

A blush suddenly crept into his cheeks. "I'm afraid I'm not very good at this sort of thing."

Charlotte tilted her head, uncertain of his meaning. Furthermore, she couldn't think of anything he was not good at. "What sort of thing?"

"You see, I've grown quite fond of you." He paused for a moment and then fixed his gaze on her. "And I want this house to be perfect for *you*."

Her heart fluttered at his earnest, humble admission.

"You have always asserted that you have no family left in Charles Town. No father, or uncle, or brother?"

She looked down and shook her head.

He reached for her hands. "Then whose permission would a gentleman seek if he wanted to ask for your hand in marriage?" A broad grin crossed his face, as if he were relieved to have finally uttered those words.

Charlotte mirrored his expression and raised her chin. "I suppose a gentleman would have to ask me directly…if he were so inclined."

His mouth twitched with a sort of nervous joy. "Then, my dear Charlotte, would you do me the honor of becoming my wife?"

Breathless, she watched him bow low to the ground. "Yes. Yes. Of course!"

"If I'd known I'd be as happy as I am in this moment, I would've asked you the moment I laid eyes on you." Beaming, he straightened to meet her gaze once more.

"Had you done that, I might have thought you were mad." She laughed.

He took her in his arms and kissed her in a way he never had before. "I swear that no matter what trials we endure, I will love and cherish you until the day I die."

Of that, Charlotte had no doubt.

about the author

Chrissy Lessey is a beach bum with a deep appreciation for good jokes, strong coffee, and salt air. She lives on the beautiful Crystal Coast of North Carolina where she finds endless opportunities to procrastinate and daydream. A long-time fan of rock music, Chrissy married a talented drummer. She still loves listening to him play—as long as it's not in the house. Together, they have two energetic children and an ill-mannered dog.

She enjoys connecting with her fans both in person and online. Visit ChrissyLessey.com or follow her on Facebook, Twitter, and Instagram to stay up-to-date on her latest book news and upcoming appearances.

acknowledgements

My heartfelt gratitude goes to the team at Tenacious Books Publishing for their efforts in producing this novella. Your support has been invaluable to me throughout the development of the entire Crystal Coast Series.

Special thanks to Erin and Deek Rhew for "rhewining" everything. Again.

Hats off to Jeff Lessey, Chris Alderson, Jessica Calla, and Missy Barber for managing to discover editorial issues even after I read the manuscript so many times I could recite it from memory. I'm grateful for your eagle-eyed reading.

I'd also like to thank my dog Buddy. We've written four books together now. I think he's getting quite good at it.

praise for the crystal coast series

"*The Coven* is atmospheric, intriguing, and at times deeply moving. With terrific characters, a vivid setting, and plot that clips along smartly, this book is a great read. A series to dive into!"

- Paula Brackston,
New York Times Bestselling author of *The Witch's Daughter*

"Interesting characters, well-written dialogue, and a rich history combine to make *The Coven* by Chrissy Lessey an engrossing read."

-5 star review from Reader's Favorite

"Chrissy Lessey's historical urban fantasy, *The Secret Keepers* is a delightful story of perseverance, determination, and sisterhood."

-Jessica Calla,
author of *Summer Maple Wallace: A Novel*

"Lessey's story is both heartwarming and surprisingly believable."

- C.H. Armstrong,
author of *The Edge of Nowhere*

"The secret world of a witch who will stop at nothing to save her son. Splendidly written. A FINALIST and highly recommended."

-Wishing Shelf Book Awards

"Chrissy Lessey's *The Hunted* is a tale of loss, love and learning how the power of good versus evil can be devastating, but will bring out the best in those who are the most innocent and free of darkness. A wonderful tale that embraces the magic of the author's storytelling and combines high tension, dark enemies and the quest to survive in a world that has become as dangerous as a riled viper in a pit. A well told tale that relies on its characters and their inherent good as opposed to gore and guts."

- Tome Tender Book Blog

"Like its predecessors, *The Beacon* is addicting entertainment that delivers one hundred percent and wraps up the series perfectly. A must read for fans of contemporary fantasy, women's fiction, literary fiction, and hell, anyone looking for a book they can't put down."

-Steph Post,
author of *Miraculum*